AN HONOURABLE DEATH

IAIN CRICHTON SMITH

AN
HONOURABLE
DEATH

MACMILLAN
LONDON

First published 1992 by
MACMILLAN LONDON LIMITED
a division of Pan Macmillan Publishers Limited
Cavaye Place London SW10 9PG
and Basingstoke

Reprinted 1992

Associated companies in Auckland, Budapest, Dublin,
Gaborone, Harare, Hong Kong, Kampala, Kuala Lumpur,
Lagos, Madras, Manzini, Melbourne, Mexico City, Nairobi,
New York, Singapore, Sydney, Tokyo and Windhoek

ISBN 0-333-56801-X

A CIP catalogue record for this book is available from the
British Library

Typeset by Pan Macmillan Production Limited
Printed by Billing & Sons Ltd, Worcester

ACKNOWLEDGEMENTS

Some of the books I have consulted are as follows:

Campbell, David, *Major-General Hector A. Macdonald, CB, DSO, LLD*, London: Hood, Douglas and Howard, and Andrew Melrose, E.C, 1899.

Chevenix-Trench, Charles, *Charley Gordon, the Eminent Victorian Re-assessed*, London: Allen Lane, 1978.

Coates, Thomas E. G., *Hector Macdonald or the Private who became a General*, London: S.W. Partridge and Co., 1900.

Daiches, David (ed.), *Edinburgh, a Travellers' Companion*, London: Constable, 1986.

Elton, Lord (ed.), *General Gordon's Khartoum Journal*, London: William Kimber, 1961.

Fraser, Duncan, *Edinburgh in Olden Times*, Montrose: Standard Press, 1976.

Friseal, Ailean, *Eachunn nan Cath*, Glasgow: Gairm Publications, 1979.

Johnson, Peter, *Gordon of Khartoum*, London: Patrick Stephen, 1985.

Keppel-Jones, A., *South Africa*, London: Hutchinson University Library, 1949.

Macleod, Kenneth I. E., *The Ranker*: published by the author, (1976).

A Victim of Fate: published by the author, (1978).

Magnus, Philip, *Kitchener, a Portrait of an Imperialist*, London: John Murray, 1958.

Minto, C. S., *Victorian and Edwardian Edinburgh from Old Photographs*, London: Batsford, 1973.

Montgomery, John, *Toll for the Brave*, London: Max Parrish, 1963.

Nutting, Antony, *Gordon, Martyr and Misfit*, London: Constable, 1966.

Royle, Trevor, *Death before Dishonour, the True Story of Fighting Mac*, Edinburgh: Mainstream, 1982.

    The Kitchener Enigma, London: Michael Joseph, 1985.

Warner, Philip, *Kitchener: The Man Behind the Legend*, London: Hamish Hamilton, 1985.

Ceylon – Zeylanicus, London: Elek Books, 1970.

I would also like to thank the staff of the Queen Mother Library, Aberdeen, for being most helpful and kind and patient with me during the time I was researching the story. I was staggered by their efficiency.

I would like to stress that although I have done much reading for this book, it is still a novel, and I have used my imagination particularly in delineating the relationship between Christine and Hector in Edinburgh, and in elaborating on Hector's thoughts, though within the parameters of his character as I understand it.

1

THE man walked along the corridor to Room 105, opened the door and put down his case. There was a wardrobe, a wash-basin, a chair: it was a simple, anonymous room, exactly what he wanted.

He sat down on the bed and stretched out his legs: one of them seemed to be giving him pain. He looked almost too large for the room. He was a sturdy, compact man with an extensive moustache which drooped in a curve round his mouth; his hair was cut short and formed a V on his forehead; he had big ears which projected prominently from his head. He smiled in an ironical way as he considered himself sitting in a room in a hotel in Paris. He, the son of a crofter from the Highlands of Scotland! That mirror, for instance, in which he saw himself, looked heavy and rich and imperial. Then he thought of what was happening to him, what was about to happen, and his smile faded. Lines like plough-lines furrowed his forehead.

He seemed restless, uncertain what he should do. Now and again he would get up and look down through the window on to the Tuileries Gardens. Then he would turn back again into the room, which seemed more and more like a cell. Should he stay in, should he go out? Would he be recognised, even in civilian clothes? He had seen a thin, well-dressed woman in the lounge; she had said 'Good evening' to him in English. She might have recognised him – his picture had been in the newspapers often enough – though he had registered himself without his full title. Women, however, were very quick, very perceptive, though in his spartan life he had not been of much use to them. Apart from one, of course . . .

He went to the window again and returned to the centre of the room. He felt the energy of Paris but he seemed like a prisoner. Perhaps at that very moment people were entering theatres in their cloaks and dresses. Such a romantic city, Paris, with its perfumes, sparkling lights, cafés, gardens, palaces. And its legendary freedom. The hotel itself with its lovely façade looked down on to the Tuileries.

His eyes roamed his cell again. He would have felt more comfortable in his uniform, but then he would have been easily recognised. His uniform, however, was his defence against the civilian world. Now, dressed as a civilian, it was as if he had entered a world too disordered, too loose. On the other hand his uniform hadn't saved him in the military world either. He had expected more from Roberts, more understanding, more charity, perhaps. The memory of those icy, uncomprehending eyes bothered him.

He looked at the writing-table. He went over to it as if he wished to write some letters, but then decided against it. His wife – he had seen her recently – no, there was little point in writing to her. As for his brother, how could he bring himself to tell him? He smiled at the heading on the writing-paper. Hotel Regina. As if it were Queen Victoria, dead now, but the mistress he had served in heat and cold. Different from the King with his stupid hard-boiled eyes. Again he felt restless, like a huge clumsy animal in this small room. It was hard to explain what had happened to him, the sudden ruin. His past counted for nothing now. And if they heard about it in the Highlands, why . . .

The thought of his predicament was unbearable. He could no longer stay in the room, he had to move about. He walked along the corridor until he came to Reception. Then, leaving his key behind him, he strode about the streets; he wished to walk and walk, to keep himself from thinking, to outwalk his mind. He had no idea where he was going. His mind was burning with the puzzle that tormented him, in a Paris burning with lights.

2

BEHIND the counter of the shop in Inverness, called the Royal Clan Tartan and Tweed Warehouse, stood a tall young man in black clothes who looked more like a farmer than a shop assistant. His hands were large and red, and the sleeves of his jacket rather short. He seemed healthy, raw and large. Round him were the varicoloured tweeds, tartans. He was alone in the shop.

Suddenly he left the counter (after first looking around him) and began to march up and down in a military manner, barking out commands to himself: 'Attention, right turn!' His feet clicked on the wooden floor. He saw himself surrounded by soldiers all in tartan. He imagined himself being called in front of the commander, a tall handsome man with a moustache, who said to him in tones of quiet reverence, 'You have done well, Macdonald, without you we wouldn't have taken that hill.' He flushed, trying however to feel humble and obedient.

The commander rose to his feet, put his hand on Hector's shoulder, looked deep into his eyes, and said, 'Very well indeed.' Then he pinned a medal on him. In the background there was a burst of cheering which might have been coming from the rolls of tartan all around him in the darkness.

Suddenly he heard the door opening, and turned from his dream. A smallish man with a bald head was standing at the counter. Hector smoothed down his black suit, emerging from the darkness.

'Sir,' he said.

'I was wondering,' said the small man hesitantly, 'that is to say, my wife . . . I would like to order a kilt.'

'Which tartan, sir?'

'Eh?'

'Which tartan, sir?' said Hector patiently, while at the same time a wolf was shouting insults inside his head.

'As to that, I'm not sure, you understand it's my wife's idea, to tell you the truth, something in green; I like green. I'm sure you have green tartans. My wife's favourite colour is red but I would like, I think, green.'

The man straightened for a moment. His bald head is like a cannon-ball with veins in it, thought Hector. The wolf inside his head was saying, What will this small bald man look like in a kilt?

'Excuse me a moment, sir,' said Hector, 'I've got to go next door.' And he left the shop.

He walked quickly down the street past other shops. On the opposite side of the street he saw a beggar with red blisters on his face. They looked raw and pitiful but it was said that beggars rubbed stuff on them to make them appear worse. On his breast the beggar had a large sheet of paper written for him. There were scribes who did that sort of thing for ex-soldiers, as this beggar appeared to be. From a bar he heard singing and shouting.

Then he saw the sergeant, who was standing as usual at the corner of the street, proud and strong in his Highland regalia.

'I want to join the army, Sir,' said Hector.

'How old are you?' said the sergeant.

'Seventeen, Sir,' said Hector.

'Too young, son. Come back in a year's time. Sorry.'

'Everyone says I'm tall for my age,' Hector insisted. No, he couldn't go back to that shop.

'I'm almost eighteen, Sir,' he said.

The sergeant looked at him. Yes, he did seem tall for his age. Maybe . . .

'All right, son, come with me.'

And Hector went with him and accepted the Queen's shilling.

'By the way,' said the sergeant, 'don't call me "sir". "Sir" is for officers.' No smell of beer came from his breath, though around them in the bar there was drunken singing, and soldiers in kilts. This sergeant, however, seemed very proud, glamorous, military.

'Here is a warrant,' he said, 'that you will take to Aberdeen. You will report there at Castle Hill barracks. Do you understand?'

'Yes, sergeant.' Already he was standing at attention. His heart was leaping with joy. He looked down at his black suit with contempt. It was as if his life up to this point had been a funeral.

He took his warrant and walked to the railway station. He had completely forgotten the small bald man he had left in the shop. He marched like a soldier, his back ramrod-straight.

The beggar, who had a dirty cloth round his head, put out his hand to him. Hector caught a glimpse of the word 'India' on the litany of the man's battle honours. Was he blind or pretending to be blind? Hector stared into his eyes but could see no glimmer of life. The man stared ahead of him, his hand held out, as if he were a wax figure in a shop.

For a moment Hector felt a chill, as of death itself, then he thrust a shilling into the blind man's hand.

'Now we're quits,' he said, and headed for the train.

That too was an adventure. Steam blossomed around him; other uniformed men were there, looking busy and pompous. He opened the carriage door and entered. When the train was leaving he didn't go to the window and look back at Inverness.

When he arrived at the camp he was booked in. Afterwards he was stripped naked in front of a doctor who wore a monocle. This was to make sure that he had no lice or fleas. His nakedness made him feel vulnerable and ashamed.

'You're a tall fellow,' said the doctor. Hector looked around him: most of the men were smaller than he but had larger dicks. Nor did they seem to feel vulnerable, in fact they were joking with each other, their bodies white as worms. One of them had a galaxy of spots on his chest. To be naked, however, was to be defenceless, shameful. I hate this, he thought, I can't wait to be dressed in my uniform. The monocle glared at him, the single eye of an indifferent monster, and then he was past it on his way to the stores for his clothes and blankets.

He had to parcel up his suit and send it home to his parents. This was a decisive moment, it was as if he was saying, Goodbye, I'm setting off for another world, I'm no longer the son you knew. The days of the farm are over, the days of the shop are finished. I'm sorry I didn't tell you what I was going to do but I know you wouldn't have approved. Like everyone else you think the army consists of drunken rogues and vagabonds. This is my good black suit I'm sending to you: it is a sign of the good moral world that you approve of, the tight black world that you said was the best. First I was naked, then I was clothed, then I was unclothed again. Let the dead bury their dead. I am risen again from your world into a new world. I did this on impulse and I do not regret it. My destiny is here.

Since some of the recruits were illiterate, he had to write their addresses for them.

That night he lay on a hard, uncomfortable bed staring out at the hard, brilliant moon, not at all like the autumn moon of the harvest but colder, firmer, harder, like a coin spinning through the clouds.

He was wakened at half past five in the morning by the brisk bugle. He heard mutterings, oaths, splashings of water. He made his iron bed as the others did, placing the blankets on top, tied together, then finally he folded it.

There was a smell of sweat in the barrack-room, and as he stood there shivering he saw a mountainous blanket ahead of him and realised that one of the soldiers was masturbating.

They went out on to the square where the corporal was waiting for them. The next two hours were a fury of commands. He had to learn to stand at attention, to march.

The corporal was a small man with a moustache. He seemed hostile, enraged.

'I'm standing on your hair!' he shouted at one man. 'Get it cut!'

And to another, 'You're marching like a penguin. Swing those arms!'

There were obscene references to mothers, sisters, girlfriends.

Hector hated this, he hated it in his deepest being. The corporal, stiff as a poker, had a face red as a cockerel on which his moustache quivered with a life of its own. His head seemed square, the colour of his hair was like that of a hedgehog Hector had once seen. He had been provided with this formless mass: always he had to begin again. Its formlessness offended him as his obscenities offended Hector.

Legs, arms, bodies lacked harmony. Men could not keep in step: they had the clumsiness of the civilian. They had the loose, hateful freedom of the civilian deep within them. The corporal's job was to drive out that scent, that alien perfume which was almost feminine. The men must become as firm as bayonets, they must learn the firm masculinity of machines.

The men reacted slowly to commands. They belonged to the unstructured world outside the gates with its continual crazy motions, its accidental strayings. They were dogs with devoted, beseeching looks. In their lack of harmony they were stupid.

'When I'm finished with you, your mothers won't know you,' the corporal shouted in his frenzied anger, himself brisk and compact and fearsome.

Here nothing was sacred. All must be subordinated to orders, law, tidiness. You were converted to a number: you had no gifts, talents, character of your own. It was your number that was on a charge and if there was a bureaucratic error then it was not you at all, and your charge would be dismissed.

Rage infected the air in which the men lived, rage that there wasn't a perfect, orderly world, that always somehow or other a little of the ego was left and refused to be destroyed. Rage was like the raw sunrise that inflamed the sky in the morning. The sky itself was a raw wound festering. It was a rage against disorder, and a rage of boredom.

By the left, by the left . . . The harsh, viperish voice followed them, would not leave them alone, as they tried to do their best at marching. It would be there for ever, floating out of the red dawn, raucous as a red bird. They were like sheep-dogs answering their master's whistle, thought Hector, who enjoyed the marching, as he had practised marching before,

7

often, with a Volunteer Company in Inverness. He had an army manual and studied it behind the counter in the shop in Inverness. He was not frightened; this was what he was born to do.

This was the new world in which he was to be shaped and formed, sharpened, made an instrument. The harsh voice came out of the red sunrise, in the cold of the morning, among the chilling red clouds, the working factory of the sky.

Breakfast at eight o'clock consisted of tea and bread and butter and porridge. The tables were put away, the floor swept, and there was an interval of rest until the bugle blew again for more training.

The screams were hideous, unearthly, as if men had been let loose from a madhouse. The straw man swayed as the steel pierced him.

Screaming, they came at the straw man, demented tribesmen, shrieking with hatred, nerves, fear, released anger. Some thought of the straw man as the corporal himself, some saw it as the embodiment of their deprived lives. The straw man endured it all, rape, pillage, aggression. The bayonets quivered in him, were retracted. The swaying straw man, heavy and sluggish, was burst here and there.

The furious recruits attacked him with heavy grunts, but he still remained, stubborn, blank, ironic, unyielding. It was the senseless nature of their lives.

A lieutenant with a stick under his arm paused and looked at them.

'How are they doing, corporal?' he said in a languid voice.

The corporal sprang quickly to attention and shouted, eyes staring straight ahead of him, 'Improving, SAH!'

The 'sah' seemed to echo back from the stony parade-ground.

'Good, good,' said the lieutenant. 'Carry on, corporal.'

Idiot, thought the corporal. Ignorant long drink of water. He thought of himself as the ardent worker while the officer

dummy looked on. The languid man had gazed only for a
moment at the bristly, uncouth straw man.

When the lieutenant had drifted away the corporal turned back
to his uniformed lunatics who were still screaming, and shouted,
'Come on, you little men! Get it in! GET IT IN!' His voice too
was a high scream, as if he was a seagull screaming over a waste
of water, as if he himself was a woman being raped.

After dinner there was a game of football in which Hector, who
was a good footballer, took part.

'Holy Jesus, you're a big fella,' said a little Irishman to him.
'Where are you from?'

'The Black Isle,' said Hector.

'And where is that when it's at home?'

Hector told him.

'I'm from the West of Ireland myself, and I wish to Jesus I
was back there. Why did you join up?'

Hector told him.

'You mean you had a job and left it?' said the Irishman in
amazement. 'You must have a potato for a head.'

Hector smiled and joined in the game. The seemingly casual
yet tactical patterns of football enchanted him.

'Goal!' someone shouted.

'Jesus, would you believe it, we've scored,' said the Irishman.

They were ready to go out. They were polishing their boots, their
belt-buckles, they were sleeking back their hair. Hector listened
vaguely to their talk. All they talked about was women and drink:
they were entirely physical. At first this had amazed him but now
he had grown used to it. Among the Gaelic voices he could hear
English ones, Irish ones.

'I'll give her a touch of the bayonet tonight,' he heard someone
saying. There was a laugh from men who had worked and suffered
together and who knew the real meaning of the joke, for whom
it was not just a simile. Already in their conversations they were

beginning to become a unit, a company, though they themselves perhaps did not realise it.

Out of the air around them they were gathering the material for story, badinage, legend. They lived off the random leavings of the day and created their heroes and demons from them. Mornings rose and made them what they would become: they collected like cows under rain. Witticisms rose from the bare square: myths were made by men such as these from the scatterings they found about them. They inspected the plans that had been laid out for them, chewed at them endlessly, tasted them, confronted the straw man in the raw air of morning.

They talked a lot about their corporal. At times they hated him, at other times they might say, 'Well, he's got a job to do, hasn't he?' They pretended they didn't like the army but secretly delighted in their new skills. They talked contemptuously of civilians.

And laughing and joking they set off, picking up what they could, surviving.

'Not coming, Hector?'

No, he would stay and read and maybe have a beer. There was no whisky on the camp but there was beer. There was so much to learn and this was his destiny. For themselves they had no destinies, they lived from minute to minute, from hour to hour. They weren't abstract people, large words like 'destiny' were not part of their vocabulary.

Sometimes they would talk about God, though. Their arguments were naive, without rigour.

'There must be something,' they would say. 'Where did we come from, then?' Then someone would say, 'Christ knows where the "Hammer" [this was the RSM] comes from,' and then they would laugh. Their observations about God were like bits of straw that came from the straw man. Logic was alien to them.

Then after talking about religion they might start talking about ghosts.

'Ghosts have no bodies, of course,' someone would say sagely, drawing at his pipe. 'They're supposed to be spirits.'

10

'How can you see them, then?' someone else would ask, and there would be a long pause.

'Well, it's like gas, you see,' and smoke would pour from the pipe.

One day after a long march they trooped in to hear the languid lieutenant talk to them about regimental history. He took off his cap and pointed with a stick to the blackboard on which he had written 'The Gordon Highlanders'.

'The Gordon Highlanders,' he told them, 'were raised in 1794 by the fourth Duke of Gordon. There is a story that the Duchess would offer a personal kiss to every man who joined up. In the Peninsula War they fought in every battle and after the death of Sir John Moore at Corunna they adopted the use of black buttons on their spats as a form of mourning. They fought at Quatre Bras and at Waterloo. At Waterloo the heavy cavalry charged the French lines and as the Royal Scots Greys advanced into the attack, the men of the Gordons clung on to the troopers' stirrups, so eager were they to fight.'

There was a snore from the back of the room. The lieutenant hesitated, his pointing stick paralysed in his hand. Then he turned and his face was red and swollen with rage. His eyes protruded from his head and he screamed like a woman.

'Sergeant, there's a man there sleeping. I can SEE him. Put him on a charge. Immediately. This instant.'

'SAH!' said the sergeant, standing up and marching over to where the man was twitching out of sleep and entering the room again in his raw naked wakefulness.

The rest sat up straighter in their seats ... Quatre Bras, Waterloo, black buttons, cavalry, and watched, themselves trembling, the lieutenant trembling with rage.

Hector loved drill and was good at it, as he was at all the tasks he had to do, including shooting and PT. But it was drill that attracted him most and most moved him. There was about it a mystique, a definiteness, an accuracy that enchanted him. The barked commands evoked exact responses from him. He could see as he looked around him shapelessness becoming form, a pure, severe order emerging. Thus geometry created perfection, as if the men were being played like a strange instrument. The best would withdraw from the worst, the inadequate, the wounded ones, who were often made to run round the square with their rifles held above their heads. A pride stirred in the successful man. Perhaps this was the first thing he had succeeded at. To be successful was to become part of the harmony, success in itself was not an individual thing. The pride swelled to the music of bagpipes, to parades: it became swagger, laughter. The men and the marching became a mystical music. To see civilians was to see untidiness, variousness.

As they became fitter and better at drill and their other work, they became more high-spirited. The successful ones played tricks on the wounded and the vulnerable and the inefficient. They turfed them out of their beds, made fun of them. There was cruelty as well as high-spiritedness. Only it wasn't seen as cruelty, it was seen as sport, soon forgotten.

And they talked continuously about women, about their exploits with prostitutes and others. Some of them had escaped into the army because they had no money, or because they had been felons and had got into trouble with the police. They also drank a great deal.

They were purely physical beings, quite close to the animal. Hector sensed a pathos about them, felt himself separate from them. Their talk about women disgusted him.

One of the English recruits told Hector, 'What we used to do was this. We used to make up to maids in fancy houses, a couple of us. Then when they told us the mistress was out we used to take the maids upstairs and leave the door on the latch. Then the third man would come in and take the stuff. Other times we might come into a house through the roof. We used to have dolly mops to pick the pockets of drunk people. Another prank we had, two of us would pick on a gent and quarrel with him, then a third one would come along and pretend he was helping him. He would lead him to a quiet place and fleece him. We had neddies to hit people with. Then we used to rob children, ones who had been sent on errands. That's what we called skinning, even taking their clothes. The dolly mops were good at that, some of them looked like angels but wicked as hell underneath. It was a great time while it lasted, lived off the fat of the land. But the peelers nearly had us one day, so I joined the army. I'm not all that keen on it, but what else is there to do?'

This was a whole new world to Hector and he listened with wonder. In his own area no one stole anything, though people were not rich. Doors were never locked. The Bible told them not to steal and that commandment was adhered to. To steal was to be ostracised: it was utter disgrace. But there, in that English world, were men who knew little about the Bible and who, if they had, would have ignored its laws. They scrambled for life in seething warrens, where there were rats as well as people. They preyed on the young and innocent, and women were as bad as men. Stealing was in fact their profession as his had been to work in a shop.

They had deceived, cheated, maimed and perhaps killed.

There came a time when they grew almost friendly with the corporals and sergeants, who would borrow money from them and never pay it back. Or the men would buy them drinks, for the corporals and sergeants never paid for anything. Why, they were human after all and would joke with them. It must be hard to make people like themselves into soldiers; it must be boring starting all over again with every new intake. And then all this hard training was necessary to prepare them for battle, it was in their own interests. And you couldn't say that they didn't know their jobs. No, in general they all fitted into this new scheme, they and the sergeant and the corporal, they had come through a difficult time together and they had triumphed. They now had a certain security.

They were endlessly fascinating to Hector with their feckless-ness, their flashes of pride, their cruelty, their generosity. They never had any money for as soon as they got it they spent it.

They never read books because many of them were illiterate. Yet they could never be cheated of a penny on pay day. The Highlanders themselves were among the most educated, and Hector would speak to them in Gaelic.

Some of the soldiers lived in a fantasy world. They made up stories about their previous lives, their families. One of them, a small fellow with a pale, pinched face, insisted that his father was a doctor. He described his father's practice in great detail. They lived in a big house in the middle of parkland. When he was a boy he hunted for rabbits and hare and fished for salmon in a stream. His fantasies were well researched and not believed by anyone. However, some of them lived off their fantasies as off some exotic food, unlike the food that they actually ate.

At one stage when they hated their endless drill and the sadism of the corporal, one of them said that he knew of a man in the town who would beat him up. He would come up to him when he was in the pub, pick a quarrel and break his arms, and then they would be free of him. But nothing ever happened of course, although for a while they waited hopefully for the big fight. The corporal, however, continued to rule the square as he had always done.

There was also a man who read books all the time. He had big round glasses and his books were either about the Church or about history. His life was one sustained torture: he was always on charges, he couldn't march in step, but his books kept him going until one day someone tore them up. He would wander about the camp in a dazed state until he was dismissed from the army since he couldn't get through his training successfully.

There was another man who told them that there were mysterious higher-ups they could complain to. These higher-ups would overrule the corporals and sergeants and even put them on charges and dismiss them. These higher-ups might be political, they would have the interests of the men at heart: actually the sergeants and corporals were terrified of them. The men would listen to this barrack-room lawyer like little children looking for help in the dark.

Although they could be cruel the men had sudden flashes of

generosity. And they were especially fond of children whom they regarded as symbols of purity. When they heard that a child belonging to one of the men had to go into hospital, they clubbed together so that toys could be bought for him.

At one stage one of them said, 'That corporal had to become friendly. It was to save his own life. Else we would have put a bullet into his back first time we were in action.' He told a story of a bullying sergeant who had disappeared from a troop-ship: his body had never been found. Obviously he had been thrown over the side by the men.

Some nights, because of his guilt at running away to the army without telling his parents, Hector would have nightmares. In one in particular he was standing trial in the Free Church school he had attended. He was barefoot and he felt cramped inside his desk where somehow or other he stood at attention. His interrogator was wearing a black minister's robe.

'Tell me the story of the Prodigal Son,' the voice ordered. Hector stuttered but not a word came from his mouth.

Suddenly his father was in the classroom as well: he was in fact building one side of the classroom like the mason he was. His raw red hands fumbled at the bricks and his head hung down. Hector felt sorry for him. But the inflexible voice went on, 'You have sinned. And you will be sent to hell.' There was a fire in the room with a pail of peats beside it.

Nevertheless, instead of the fires of hell, Hector felt the most intense cold. He was standing on an icy hill looking down into a field where people were moving about in clothes as brown as the earth. There was a high wind: he tried to shout to them but they weren't hearing him. Either they were deaf or they were ignoring him. They carried on with whatever tasks they were doing, some smoking, some eating, some simply walking about.

'What is the chief end of man?' a voice asked him.

He thought and thought. The answer was on the tip of his tongue but he couldn't find it.

He looked down at his legs. He was standing in the most

intense cold and he was barefoot. There was snow round his feet.

The scene changed again according to the logic of dreams. This time he was standing in a shop serving a customer. He was swathed in tartan which covered him from head to toe.

'There you are, sir,' he said to the man who had a red angry face. 'That suit is far too big for me,' the man said. 'You should know that. I should send for the manager; you are totally incompetent. Anyone would see at a glance that this suit is too big. And look at it. It's got holes in it. What sort of shop is this? What do you think I am? Do you think I am a fool?' And he thrust his large red angry face at Hector, who actually felt a rain of spittle on his cheeks. 'I'll send for the manager!' the man shouted.

'I am the manager,' said Hector.

'You the manager! You're far too young and in any case you don't know your Bible. Look at that suit. It's moth-eaten, and it is falling apart.'

Hector held out his hand for the suit and, true enough, it disintegrated like a spider's web in his hands. He stood staring down at it in amazement.

'And you advertise yourselves as the best shop in Inverness too,' said the man furiously. 'You will have to be reported.'

'I could have sworn,' said Hector, still puzzled.

'You think that because you are wearing a coat of many colours yourself,' said the man, 'you can sell your customers anything. I am going to send for the police. I will make sure that you will be prosecuted. And what's that you have been reading? That's not a Bible. I don't know what book that is.'

Suddenly Hector felt the most intense and passionate anger.

'Stand at attention when you're speaking to me!' he shouted in a rage. 'And pick your feet up! Who do you think you are, coming into this shop in such a slovenly manner? Look at all this, it's clean, do you understand, and you come in here with your dirty boots and order me about. And look at these buttons. They're not even polished. I may be poor but this is my shop. It's the best stuff there is.'

And the customer began marching up and down, entangled

and blinded by tweeds and tartans, while Hector poked at him with a ruler, barking orders at him.

Hector woke up to find himself entangled in the blankets. He was sweating and trembling. He forced his mind to watch the men moving in mystical manoeuvres on the square. Slowly he was calmed by the complex configurations. The personae of his dream receded one by one, and he was at peace.

3

THE sea boiled around them. The ship butted into the water and rose again: sometimes it seemed as if it would never rise. There was an ancient creaking from it. In the depths of the ship as in the depths of hell, sick, frightened, green-faced, wishing they were dead, were hundreds of soldiers. The water drummed and raced along beside them. Many of them had never been on a ship before. The water was white, lead-coloured, grey. Sickness was everywhere, like a green sticky fungus which clung to the decks. You stepped into it, slithered and almost fell, while, at the same time, the ship itself suddenly plunged or veered. The wind howled, the ship reeled. But the worst of it was when it descended into the waves and you waited, praying for it to rise. Perhaps this time it wouldn't, perhaps this time the ancient arthritic wood would refuse. Perhaps this time you would drown in a salty grave.

What would it be like? thought Hector, who, with another recruit called Robertson, was a salt-water corporal – not a substantive rank, indeed as transitory as the sea-water itself. This waste of waters, threatening, indifferent, with such enormous, frightening power, what would it be like to be sucked into it? Once, as he stood beside a recruit who was being sick, his face greenish in the stormy light, he stared out, almost hypnotised by the waves. The soldier gagged, was sick on Hector's polished boots, then poured the rest into the plentiful sea. God dammit, you've spoiled my boots, thought Hector, and for a moment he was angry, but his anger seemed so tiny in the middle of that maelstrom that it subsided quickly. In any case, what did these waters care about shiny boots, ceremonies, passing-out parades, regulations? The power of the sea was immense, unimaginable. You wouldn't last a minute in it. The water was like an infinitude of roofs collapsing.

It seemed as he stared around him that the men lying there could not be soldiers. They stared apathetically downwards, some of them even prayed, some of them moaned, some of them tried to light pipes to keep themselves from gagging but couldn't manage to, some of them retched, bringing up green bile. The Bay of Biscay, stormy, vicious, reflected green light on their faces. The whine of the wind shook them with terror. Surely it was better to be dead than to suffer like this?

There was no need to discipline anyone, the wind and the storm did that. Sometimes there might be a sudden rancorous bickering but most of the time the men were resigned, slumped and half sleeping: there was hardly enough room for them to turn. And the sea rising and falling, so that their stomachs seemed to rise and fall with it.

And even in that despair Hector felt the need to keep himself tidy and smart, as if to do so was to win against the sea. At times he felt sheer undiluted terror as the ship burrowed deep into the water, as he heard the blank echo of the waters. This time . . . this time . . . But slowly, slowly the ship came up, struggling painfully against the burden of the water. Nevertheless it was best to remain as clean and tidy as one could. That was a triumph over the elements.

And then one day there was bright colour and they were riding through the Red Sea. This time there wasn't the same motion, but it was replaced by a heat such as hardly any of them knew could exist. It was a foretaste of hell itself. There was no shelter from it anywhere.

Sweat poured from them like water. The sea burned and coruscated. The sun dried up the sickness, it reverberated from their heads as if they were so many bells, they felt as if they were boiling inside their clothes. They were dazzled. They longed for water, they longed for a cool place, even a church: the heat almost drove them demented, especially at noon when it seemed like a relentless interrogator, pouring down its ruthless rays.

On and on they sailed, cursing, burning, itchy. And the

infinite sea was around them, almost clanging like bronze, the light flashing off it in millions of sparkles.

But at night a million stars were clear above them. Sometimes they would look up at the moon and a longing for home would seize them. It was the same moon, wasn't it, everywhere? But this moon of exile would make them think of home, provincial, local. A kind of nostalgic humming would rise from them, a curious, unstudied music, as if they were aware of a perfect moderate light, but somewhere else. This coin flung into the sky attracted them. How beautiful it was, until, later on, the barbaric sun would rush into the sky with red, lurid light. They stared helplessly at its burning cannon-ball, like dumb dogs.

Their mouths became swollen, they searched for shelter but there was none. The deck was burning below them. Ravaged, itchy, light as in delirium, they floated on.

India, thought Hector, what is it? He remembered the map in the little hut of the schoolroom, so much of it coloured a blatant red. Elephants, mountains, bazaars, temples, huge crowds of people, rivers, surely that was India? Animals of all kinds, that was India. Jungles, tigers, people carrying water-jugs on their heads. He searched the recesses of his mind, seeing at the same time Mr Treasurer indicating the map with a long pointer, while a boy at the back shuffled his big tackety boots.

Women with veils, was that India or not? Crocodiles, did they have crocodiles in India? But jewellery, he remembered that there was jewellery. Mr Treasurer was pointing at the glowing map on a cold day in Ross-shire, as if the fire that emanated from it warmed him in his black clothes. And now he himself was on his way to India. It seemed impossible to him. Yet it was real, it was waiting for him, huge, mysterious, unfathomable, ungovernable.

Poor Mr Treasurer in his ill-fitting black suit, he would never see this treasure. Poor Mr Treasurer, cradling his head on bad days like a mottled globe. Poor Mr Treasurer in his little religious hut with his fire in the winter to which they all brought a peat to keep themselves and him warm.

And India burning ahead of him, strange, unearthly.

'It's not so bad,' said the sergeant to Hector, 'apart, that is, from the heat and the cholera. And there's dysentery, of course, which gives you the shits: you've got to run like hell. But the native wallahs do most of the work for you in the heat. And there's punkahs to keep you cool. And then there's the women.'

And he smiled meditatively.

'And the carvings on their temples. You should see their carvings. Cor, women with big tits. Fellows with big cocks. And at it too, you know. You know what I mean.

'Winter's best, summer's hell. All these bloody flies. And you've got mosquito nets, else you'll get malaria.'

His grizzled head was square and solid in the burning light.

'But you should see the cocks. Big as . . . you couldn't say how big they was. Beautiful women, obedient, you know.'

And it was as if for a moment something domestic hovered about him.

'Tigers there are and wild boars. The officers, you know, hunt for them. The likes of us don't.

'Dangerous too they are, them wild pigs. Come at you like lightning. And birds too, like peacocks, you should see their colours, all the colours you can think of. And the flowers.'

He tried to explain what India was like but it was too much for him. His cheeks, bell-like and bronzed, shone out of the ancient yet infinitely attractive land. How could he tell of the writhing bodies of the temples, the colours of the skies, the rivers, the ports, the dust? The wild hogs which came out of the jungle among the fresh burning flowers. The earth cracking, sometimes winds scorching you as if you were standing close to a fire. The swarms of flying ants which could devour anything. The wide esplanade of Bombay, and its harbour full of ships. The bazaars there with their ivory, spices, rhinoceros hides . . .

India got into your blood with its mysteriousness, its changing lights, the apparent endlessness of its time. And also its spare northern world, towering, cold, icy. The country almost overwhelmed you. Suddenly he shouted angrily, 'Move your arses, go on, move!'

*

And Hector learned about India as well. Sometimes the quarters were overcrowded and poorly ventilated. In the hot weather there was nothing for the men to do except play endless games of cards, or visit the brothels.

But it was the wives of the privates Hector was sorry for, the ones who chose to accompany their men in that hellish climate of the plains. They would haggle in the native bazaars and get drunk, as their children died around them or rolled in the dirt around the barracks. When their husbands were away, the women betrayed them with other men. They were sometimes beaten; some of them were very young. They calculated that if their husbands were killed they would at least get a pension.

Hector felt sorry for them. The officers, however, were a chosen race. They could take six months' leave and go off to the hills and hunt. They had hounds and horses. They would boast of their kills of tigers. And generally they didn't care for their men. There was an enormous gap there which nothing could bridge. What could an officer have to say to a young drunken wife mourning the death of a child in remorseless India? Hector was glad he hadn't married and brought a woman to this country. For the days passed more wearily for them than for the men, who were sometimes on active service and in the cooler months taking part in military exercises.

Hector wasn't lonely in those years. He played football with the men when the weather allowed it; he read and learned Urdu; he leaped from corporal to colour-sergeant. He loved the square-bashing in the cool of the morning before the sun made it impossible to move. He was a colour-sergeant in his twenties. His company was the best in the battalion. This mystique of drill was to him what their religion was to the Indians. It was a way of transforming the poor mortal flesh, of submitting it to an almost immortal law, of transforming the body as they transformed the soul. It was order, it was a way of keeping the jungle at bay. Parades were rites, they were the ornate ceremonies of his religion. And for inspiration there were the bagpipes. He could never grow tired of disciplining the body, of making it into a predestined instrument. And the soldiers became more and more what he wanted them to become. Some of them might be rebels, outlaws, but many were unified in this mystical bond. They swaggered and were proud, though of course they were always foul-mouthed, and spent their leisure time in the bazaars and brothels.

And sometimes at night Hector dreamed of more complexities, further geometrical intricacies, as if he were refining some theology of his own which had replaced the one he had learned in Sunday School.

Often he pitied the men, and sometimes even admired them. Somehow under these conditions they survived and often created a protection of jokes as one would a mosquito net against the sharp insects of the night. He would hear them trying to talk to the Indians who were employed to do most of the fatigues.

'Hey you, shit wallah!' they would shout, or, 'You haven't tied my cravat!' Their courage was endless, their instinct for survival admirable.

Twice Hector went to great parades. One was when the Prince of Wales visited Lahore. A hundred Gordons with pipes and drums were to be part of the Guard of Honour. Hector was in command of the detail assigned to guard the tent of the future King. The preparations for that Guard of Honour were of course of the most exacting kind, and Hector enjoyed them.

And there was another great parade as well, the following year when Victoria was made Empress of India. This was at Delhi, and there were 1,600 soldiers there. There were fireworks, sports, kilted Highlanders, tents, the marvellous shimmering colours of the robes of the native rulers – satin, velvet, cloth of gold – trumpets, a kaleidoscope of sight and sound. The officers of the company had to buy a pavilion and lots of champagne. (The Pearl Mosque was at Delhi; on its north and south arches are written in Persian the words, 'If there be heaven on earth, it is here, it is here.')

As Hector watched the elephants ornamented with gold and silver, and the brilliant profusion of the fireworks, as he also remembered Lahore with its Soldiers' Garden – rustic seats, a labyrinth, a menagerie, a coffee shop – he thought, I am happy in my work: this is the happiest time of my life. He was not a prolific spender; he was poised at one of the peaks of his career. He was at that moment when one gets up in the morning with an excitement that cannot be focused, that cannot be quite controlled, that is almost painful, when the world is pure and perfect and sufficient, when one is supremely good at doing what one does, when one suffers from an excess of joy, when no rust of envy has yet touched what one is, in an almost eternal present; a peak which life itself may cloud over, but there is no turning back: life must proceed. There is a moment when the old order changes not because it is bad but because it is insufficient, when to retain it is to maintain a malignancy.

Many of the officers were in debt, but Hector was not. He was popular, fit, perfectly adjusted to his work in a land more spectacular and sensuous than any he had ever known, but always aware of his duties. Hector did not have to put on a show of any kind: he had his own part in the Imperial machine and he was happy with it.

So this was Hector, as he watched the many-coloured fireworks exploding in waterfalls of light, before he had yet fought, before he had come face to face with the demons of that insecure continent, when he would be either destroyed or further defined.

4

I T WAS among the mountains of the North-West frontier that Hector would learn to know himself, while understanding little of the intricacies of high politics, of Afghanistan, of the Russian bear that might break into the plains of India. High politics were not his concern, yet in their own way they were as much a dance as parade drill: they demanded as much subtle configuration. Neither the bear nor the lion must be allowed to range too far, and certainly they must not swallow Afghanistan.

There had been missions to Afghanistan before and there had been changing tactical support for its princes. The Afghans were a proud, treacherous, independent race: in the 1840s they had destroyed General Elphinstone by treachery. He died in May 1842, racked with gout, dysentery and perhaps the visions of those terrible scenes in the Khyber for which he had been partially responsible. Now they had murdered Major Cavagnari, the most recent emissary. And they must be punished to make it quite clear to them that the British Empire could not tolerate such deeds. They must be taught to fear the lion's roar. General Roberts had listened wearily to the speeches at the farewell dinner to Cavagnari and had leaned across to a fellow guest, saying, 'That fool is doomed. They don't fear us enough yet.' But a punitive expedition was on the march and in it the Gordons marching to the sound of pipes and drums.

This was a country of snake-like passes and high mountains. It was intimidating, ferocious, inhuman and yet extraordinarily beautiful with profound hazy depths and changing colours of violet, purple and blue, and at the top the snow. Among these mists crouched an enemy whom they had to confront, a pitiless enemy who would fight to the death.

Under the command of Captain MacCallum and Lieutenant Grant, 100 men including those of Hector's company were sent to occupy the fort at Kurdiga.

It was a graveyard of camels: large naked teeth in the middle of naked skulls, a kaleidoscope of bones, and an almost unbearable stench. This was an ancient, careless, brutal mortality. They stood among that devastation, some of the men retching and being violently sick. It was negligent death on a large scale, among the towering mountains of mist and snow. It was not yet the death of men but a foretaste of it. Hector put his hand to his mouth, feeling the green bile rising, his stomach churning, stepping among the cemetery of bones.

MacCallum was training his field-glasses on the hills. They looked like the protruding eyes of camels.

'There's Afghans up there,' he said. 'How many would you say?' His face looked greenish and sick.

The Afghans wavered in the glass like microbes under a slide, active, malignant.

'I'd say about a thousand, sir,' said Hector. 'Perhaps even more.' Immediately they thought of the main army under Roberts winding its way through the snake-like passes.

It was clear that this was an ambush.

Lieutenant Grant was sent with some men to warn Roberts not to enter the pass. Hector was sent with some Gordons and forty-five Sikhs under the command of Jemadar Sher Mohammed Khan onto the hillside. (Sher Mohammed Khan was a native non-commissioned officer, a jemadar.) For the first time Hector was to be in battle. Above them were the Afghans, seemingly impregnable. A frontal attack was out of the question.

Hector cast desperately about for help from the countryside. He saw a stream pouring through the glen and led his men across it to the other side, sheltered from the Afghans. They climbed invisibly until they were above the enemy, their boots clattering among stones. His men were a thin, pitiful, colourful line making its way towards the foe. Then they were in the open: the Afghans saw them and charged, shouting 'Allah, Allah!'. 'Allah' echoed back from the blue hills. The enemy with their bearded faces were racing towards them waving swords, knives.

Hector stood firm there in the ghostly radiance of his drill-book. 'Don't fire!' he heard himself shouting. 'Not yet, not yet!' The words echoed hollowly back from the mountains. The pause seemed to last for ever. In their belted wide trousers the Afghans were running towards them, their faces contorted with hate. The straw man leaped into Hector's mind, ripped and mutilated. But these weren't straw men, these were men who hated him and his force with a malignant hatred. And yet even in that noise and in the grip of that endless pause, he felt himself cool and clear-headed, so much so that he noticed that a finger was missing from the right hand of one of the advancing enemy. But he did not fear, there seemed to be a stop-watch ticking in his head. Soon, soon he would release the men from their fixed bondage.

'Now!' he shouted. The bearded faces were closer and closer.

The concentrated fire echoed back from the hills. The bearded faces were falling away, gaps were opening, they were breaking, blood decorated their breasts with its sudden red: he saw astonished eyes, collapsing men stopped dead in their leaps. It was as if they had come up against a solid wall.

'Charge!' he shouted, and his men advanced. The Afghans were breaking before that determined, orderly movement. The bayonets plunged into the straw man from whom, however, blood flowed. There were screams of terrifying intensity: his own coolness had become madness. It was as if he had gone berserk. He was stabbing into flesh and then into air.

Then in the midst of stabbing he saw that they were gone. Bodies were lying on the ground, his bayonet was red with blood. The blood ran along it like a weird sheath.

Dazedly he looked around him. His eyes fastened on the body of an Afghan which lay at his feet, the arms outspread, the empty eyes staring up at the sky, where some birds were beginning to hover. Around him was a holocaust of celebration which echoed and echoed as if in a mad theatre. The eye of the dead Afghan both glared and winked at him, imperious, distant, and yet as if in a conspiracy with him. It was confused with the eyes of the camel, icy-cold.

So this was death, this eye. He shivered, looking at it.

The soldiers were dancing around, waving their rifles. They had won, they had come through, as he had. So this was what war was like. It hadn't been as hard as they had imagined. At a critical moment some power, if you were lucky, took over. Hector thought, I must be cooler than this, more like a workman with his tools.

It did not occur to him that General Roberts had seen the sharp violent action or that he was beginning to become a star, jagged and brilliant in the hills of Afghanistan.

Despatches *15 October*

... The energy and skill with which this party was handled reflected the highest credit on Colour-Sergeant Macdonald, 92nd Highlanders, and Jemadar Sher Mohammed Khan, 3rd Sikhs. But for their excellent service on this occasion it might probably have been impossible to carry out the programme of the march ...

This took place at Hazar Darakht – the Pass of a Thousand Trees. In the geometry of mountains, that was its name.

On 5 October the army came to Charasia, in the valley of the Logar. It was a beautiful little village nestling among orchards and gardens watered by the melting ice from the hills. A rough line of mountains rose behind it. To the south there was a steep descent where the river Logar ran between the mountains and rough steep hills on the other side. This was the narrow pass of Sang-i-nawishta, about five or six miles from Kabul. The battle which occurred there was won after a deadly struggle.

Hector himself was not in this battle. He and some Gordons under Colonel Parker were defending the base camp when some Afghans began firing on them from above. The Gordons had to climb on their hands and knees until the Afghans were cleared from the peaks and broke in disorder. And the way was now clear to Kabul, Hector having distinguished himself in two actions and come for the second time to the attention of General Roberts.

*

28

The bodies of the Afghans twisted in the cold wind. Were they the ones who had killed Cavagnari? Who knew or could know? Of course they had pleaded innocence, gone on their knees, pointed to tearful families, but they would have done that even if they had been guilty. Who wants to die? And in the end, as far as the occupying power was concerned, what did it matter? One Afghan was like another; how could you tell them apart?

Roberts had the executions carried out. Punishment was an abstract thing, it was part of a code which had to be obeyed. It had nothing to do with guilt or innocence. Pursued among the dirty narrow passageways of Kabul, men were not individuals, they were enemies of the Empire. The code of Empire, coloured blood-red, stretched out across the world. It was a red whip, a revengeful lash. If you harm the Empire, expect to die. No matter how much you weep, how much you tear your hair or grovel in the dust, you must die, for this is nothing to do with you personally. This is an army, we are the instruments of justice.

And so as morning after morning Afghans were brought out to be hanged, soldiers sat and watched the slaughter, smoking their pipes. It was their theatre, an entertainment.

And let it be said that Hector sat there at that red theatre sustained by his own code which was the code of the Empire. He too acted as one of the indifferent judges. He saw nothing wrong with it, though he was a Highlander. He was one of those spawned by Culloden who was to serve an Empire which had killed his own people.

Sometimes, however, in the face of an individual Afghan one might see pride, contempt, a ferocious will which twitched uncontrollably even against the rope. Or a single face might rest for a moment in the mind. Perhaps it had a scar, perhaps it had only one eye, perhaps it was flame-red, as if from fire. Or an Afghan might scratch his head before the rope was put around it as if he were feeling some obscure itch.

Every morning there was a new group. They hung like crows against the horizon even after their last frantic tremble, their legs rotating. The law, absolute yet illegal, rigid yet rough and ready, hoisted them to that horizon. Wives and children might howl, but the law was inflexible. It was even more inflexible

29

than that rope which did not indeed hang in the form of a question. Interrogations, alibis were not enough, were irrelevant. Did those who were hanged know Cavagnari? Had they indeed seen him?

From intricate ancient poor streets they were taken, from the poor clay houses, briefly sentenced and hanged. They were hanged because the power of their guns had failed against the power of Roberts' guns. They were hanged because they had been driven from their hills by superior fire-power.

And Hector too watched them being hanged. They had killed some of his men, his comrades. They were cruel, vicious, treacherous. Their women plunged daggers into the wounded when they found them helpless on the battlefield. Then they plundered them. They were animals, nothing more.

Their bodies twisted in the red sun. This carnival of death would teach them once and for all. There were 50,000 people in Kabul and they were the chosen ones.

Some were tied to cannon muzzles and blown apart. Informers came and bowed, pleading for money. Who knew what private feuds were being settled by the British rope? By what casual betrayal, by what bribes, by what corrupt negotiations was the Empire sustained?

Nor did these casual hangings finish the vengeance. The army, after settling into their fort at Sherpur, made raids into the Afghan glens too, savage ferocious raids as Cumberland had once made into the Highlands. In valleys deserted by their occupants, villages were burned. One image which remained with Hector was some Sikhs laughing like children as they chased some hens and then in the cold night roasted them over a fire. Every hut was systematically burnt in the arctic silence of winter. What had happened to the people, how would they survive? Where were the children, the women? The Gordons in their short kilts forded two freezing rivers, the Kabul and the Darra Narkh. Sheep, cows, mules were gathered and driven back to camp.

But that wasn't the end of the affair. As if out of the very despair of that glacial hush, a new war began, led by the fanatical

Musk-i-Alam (Fragrance of the World). Soldiers making sorties from Sherpur were attacked and savaged and only just managed to reach Sherpur in time, defended by 200 Seaforths, while a Father Brown ran about the fort telling everyone who could hold a rifle to do so. Sherpur was safe but surrounded by the ragged banners of the Afghans, green or red or blue. Kabul fell into the hands of the rebels, and any British sympathisers were immediately killed. Afghan women, keening softly, moved among the bodies of the dead, cutting off the testicles and stuffing them into the mouths of the corpses.

So as Christmas approached, the British army was besieged at Sherpur, in that huge fortress with its twenty-four miles of walls, a high sharp peak rising behind it. It became clear that the Afghans would make an attack that night, using ladders to climb the walls.

On 23 December at half past five in the morning, a light flashed from the mountain of Asmai, and this was clearly the signal for the attack. Hector waited with the others, hands on his cold rifle, for another half-hour, as the light went out. At six o'clock a tremendous din of 'Allah, Allah' rose, and there was heard the noise of racing feet. Star shells from the fort bloomed, and the enemy were seen in their thousands running towards the fort bearing ladders.

Volley after volley resounded from the defenders; the enemy fell like sheaves of corn, the noise faded, and then there was silence again. How strange it was to hear that silence, thought Hector, how strange. And again that domestic scene of the Sikhs roasting the hens returned to him, as if it had some eerie significance. And also the mooing of the cows as they were turned in the direction of the fort.

He shook his head as if to clear it, thinking of the mown Afghans out in front of the fort. And a picture of his croft returned to him quite clearly: his father and brothers were setting out with scythes, the hills were all around, the hens were clucking, the cows swished flies away from themselves.

How odd all this was, the familiarity and the strangeness. This dream of a cold, distant place, this fortress with its walls, the store-houses. And the rifle smoking in his hand, and the straw man twisting and broken in the half-darkness.

But before he could think much more he heard the bugle, eerie and desolate.

Again there were sorties among the villages. Kabul was retaken, with close fighting among labyrinthine houses, if they could be called houses, and villages were burned, vineyards set on fire – and then there was Christmas, and New Year, and snowball fights, and the easy laughter of men who had survived.

And Hector was offered a commission by General Roberts, the popular general who had led them to victory.

And he accepted the commission and passed from one community to another, from the community of the common soldier to that of the officer, from him who had nothing to him who was well off, though he might have his negligent debts. He was given a dirk by one community, a sword by the other. He was twenty-seven years old; he had climbed that ladder quickly. It was cheaper to serve in India than to serve at home: war was cheaper for him than peace. But now he would have to pay for what he had received freely in the past.

He stepped amid cheering into the Officers' Mess. He had made a crucial leap, as once when a daredevil boy he used to jump from bank to bank of a wide river. He had joined a world which was not his own.

The officers welcomed him – certainly they were not snobs, and they admired courage – but it was what they were rather than what they did that was important. They had the casual code, the casual radiance of the privileged. They could sniff each other out. They knew instinctively who was one of them.

Ian Hamilton, for instance, a contemporary of Hector's, received £200 a year from his father, a colonel in the same regiment. He was paid £350 as a lieutenant out of which his Mess bills came to £270. His grandmother owned an estate around Gairloch. He had been educated at Cheam and Sandhurst.

He too admired Hector for his courage, but it was quite clear that the latter was a sergeant in officer's dress. Why, sometimes he looked at Hamilton as if he still wished to salute him. And he didn't have much to say for himself when the other officers talked about hunting, women, visits to country estates.

Hamilton, who was a pleasant young man and not at all

snobbish, pitied Hector. This was clearly not his world, though he was a grand soldier.

Hector had no memories of public schools, of that spartan existence so much in its own way like that of the army. He sometimes spoke about a croft, but God knew what he had done there. Why, thought Ian with a smile to himself, he is like a hen among a lot of peacocks. And yet, some of these other officers are pretty block-headed too. Townshend, for example, never stops talking about his dogs, and about that tiger he once came face to face with. And that boar. Bore, right enough.

It interested Ian to see how careful, how watchful Hector was, to make sure that he was doing the right thing, when such bone-headed people as Townshend did it instinctively. Why, it must be worse for him than fighting the enemy. Yet this was what the poor blighter wanted. Dazzled by the glory of a Gordon commission, he had brought this intricate agony on himself. Ian could see him waiting before he ate, looking around him, to find out which was the correct spoon, the correct knife.

And then that discussion they had – the officers – about Cicero, and how they had evaded doing their prep. Hector was totally lost. He had clearly never heard of Cicero, or of Caesar's Gallic Wars, though apparently he had picked up more Urdu than anybody else. And he had Gaelic too. Ian himself had heard some Gaelic spoken when he had visited Gairloch.

And somehow his uniform didn't suit him as well as the others' suited them. Of course they had their own tailors. Hector clearly didn't have any money. God, how I would hate this life, thought Ian. His best bet is continual active service. And his only bet, for he certainly couldn't afford to gamble. And Ian, who was a kind person, casually tried to make things as easy as possible for Hector, educating him perhaps without Hector knowing that he was doing so, trying to prevent him from retreating into that fortress of silence in which he would make no errors: as for instance in the incident of the port . . .

Anyway, like a bride, Hector had been delivered from the rough, unprivileged hands of the soldiers to the calculated generosity of the rich. From the world of the concrete he would enter the world of the abstract, and learn the complex terminology of cutlery. For him to be an officer in the Gordons was the summit of earthly ambition. If there is heaven, it is here, it is here.

Hector turned on the threshold and looked at the men he had led and at his fellow NCOs. Their flagrant warmth almost overwhelmed him. His triumph actually was theirs. Some of them saw this clearly, that he was their flag-bearer, planting his banner firmly in the centre of the Mess with its glittering glasses. As he had led them against the Afghans so now he led them in imagination into the camp of their fabulous superiors. They clapped and cheered him. The pipes played 'Cock of the North'. They bore him on their shoulders like a rare treasure.

The story among the men was that Roberts – Bobs – had offered Hector the VC or the commission and he had chosen the commission. Bobs' career too hung on his own ability: he was not rich. He was scrupulous, daring, competent. He knew he could rely on his men for they adored him. They had wakened him with drums and pipes on New Year's morning because they wanted to see him and praise him.

Hector too was blinded by the Empire. He too was dazzled by its glamour, though after all had not the army been used to control the Highlands, by taking into it the region's fittest men? This ignorance was part of his tragedy. At the moment, however, there was no sense of tragedy, except for the relatives of those who swung from the ropes or had been slaughtered in the glens or outside Sherpur.

The vultures came down from the high skies to peck at the hanged men.

The Empire was locked into its fine justice.

5

I T WAS spring in Afghanistan, a season of unearthly beauty, the glow of green vegetation still on the high mountains, orioles and hoopoes flown back from the south. The air was peaceful: the Afghans were quiet. Their torn villages, which had suffered numerous Glencoes from Roberts' army, women and children fleeing into the hills from the Sikhs intoxicated with blood and fire, waited to be healed. Christmas and New Year had passed in revelry while Afghan bodies rotted on the hills. A correspondent attached to the army had written to the London newspapers listing the atrocities committed by the military, the pitiless revenge taken in freezing temperatures. Questions were asked in Parliament: the Whigs were enraged. Roberts' answer was to expel the correspondent from Afghanistan and into India.

But now it was spring, when the geometries of winter put on flesh. The grim mountains were seething with fresh colour. The camp was busy and vibrant. A job had been done. It seemed as if the simmering Afghans were at last exhausted by the rapine that had been visited on them. Even the breezes were fragrant with victory.

General Stewart fought his way from Kandahar to Kabul to take over command. Roberts, bristling, asked to be sent back to India, but luckily for him his request was refused. General Stewart's force at Kandahar had been replaced by an inexperienced force from Bombay which was defeated at Maiwand. Kandahar was in a precarious position, needed to be relieved. Roberts asked permission to do so, from over 300 miles away with 10,000 men, among them the Gordons and Seaforths and regiments of Gurkhas and Sikhs.

*

'The men are, to say the least of it, a bit fed up,' said Lieutenant Robertson to Hector, as he poured himself a cup of coffee. 'Can't say I blame them either. They thought they might be sent to India for a spot of leave. And now they're heading for God-forsaken Kandahar. And I'll tell you another thing, old Bobs and Stewart don't get on.'

'What do you think it will be like, the march to Kandahar, I mean?' said Hector mildly.

'Hellish, old boy. Diabolical. It'll be bloody hot, that's for sure.' He stretched out his legs luxuriously. 'Still, to tell you the truth, I'll be glad to see the last of these bloody mountains. And I can't say that I liked the executions all that much, though the Sikhs seemed to take to them. Bloody vicious, the Sikhs. And the Afghans are bloody good fighters too. Hate us, of course.'

'Yes,' said Hector, 'that's right enough.'

He found it odd to listen to the easy, open manner of the 'true' officer and his way of committing himself to criticism: it was as if the mentality of the sergeant still remained with him. To him, Roberts and Stewart were higher, more glacial mountains than they were to Robertson, for instance. He eased his neck and shoulders as if the uniform were too tight for him. Sometimes he felt as if he should be saying 'sir' to Lieutenant Robertson. When would he be rid of that? The napery of the Mess seemed like freshly fallen snow.

'You mark my words,' said Robertson, 'that march will be like hell, and all for Bobs' glory. Why do you think he volunteered for it? He can't stand Stewart being in command here, not that I blame him. And he's taking a hell of a risk too. Still, maybe he'll do anything to get away from Stewart. He's used to being cock of the walk and he loves all that adulation of the common soldier, etc. As I suppose we all would, old boy. It must be heady stuff. Write home much yourself, Mac?'

'Not much. I'm not a great hand at writing.'

'Oh, I love writing. Makes me feel that I know where I've been, eh, old boy. At least I can put the address on my letter and remind myself.'

And he laughed shortly.

'I mean, all these places. Who's going to remember them? I suppose they have a meaning in their own language. But of course you speak Gaelic, don't you?'

'Yes.'

'Well, do you think we'll remember these places when we're eighty, if we ever reach that age? Do you think Hazar Darakht will ring a bell? There's a thought for you, Mac. They're not like Agincourt, are they? They'll think themselves accursed they were not here.' He laughed. Hector didn't recognise the quotation.

'I mean,' said Robertson in his momentary delight, 'the names. They're so odd.'

I will always remember Afghanistan, thought Hector. This is where I earned my commission. This is where I fought in my first real battle. Of course I'll remember it.

'You know what I'll remember best?' said Robertson. 'It was some Sikhs warming their hands at a blazing hut. Something odd about it. Laughing and chattering. What will you remember, Hector?'

Actually, what Hector remembered best was seeing an Afghan woman dragging herself through the snow, leaving spots of blood behind her. She was looking at him with bitter ferocity. It was only after she collapsed that he saw the dagger stuck in her back. But he still remembered that stare of defiant enmity through the lightly falling snow.

'The things we do for the Empire,' said Robertson. 'Still, the people lying abed might well envy our excesses.'

Apart from Hamilton, Hector preferred Robertson to most of the subalterns, who talked a great deal about hunting, their red cheeks ballooning into the Afghan day, blatant, glowing. But there was something in Robertson that he didn't understand either, a glancing, ironical way of talking.

He felt that he knew what Robertson meant about excesses, for in battle it was as if the enemy stood for devils in himself that he wished to exorcise, as if at times he was killing himself over and over in a perpetual nightmare. And then a strange enraged person would take over. The strong right arm of the sergeant flashed out of the officer's uniform. You couldn't kill a man without feeling something unless you were a beast. You had to wind yourself up to be the red devil to the foe. And often you shouted, as if fighting the straw man, as if drowning your own devilry in noise.

'Better to have no imagination at all,' said Robertson, getting to his feet. 'That's the answer. I'd better go and explain to my fodder why they're not going to India after all for a rest cure in the old brothel, why they're going to Kandahar instead. They form part of Bobs' medals.' And he laughed. 'See you, old boy.' He turned at the door. 'Who do you think Bobs prefers, the Afghans or Stewart? I wouldn't take a bet on it.' His laughter followed him out.

Hector shook himself like a dog emerging from water. Often Robertson's comments unsettled him. On the other hand he preferred them to conversations about horses and hounds. If these officers had only seen the hut in which he had been educated by Treasurer! Why, it was not much better than the Afghan huts.

And the fights they had had after school, throwing stones at each other in ragged gangs. Why, they had been like little tribesmen themselves. Imagine that, lining up and throwing stones at each other, like David and Goliath.

And the tricks they used to play to try to get off school. One day they told Mr Treasurer they had been following a ball upstream. 'First time I heard of that,' said Mr Treasurer drily. Hector himself had been the leader. But that had been when he was very young.

And one of these days he must write to Mr Mackay, his employer in Inverness. He shouldn't have run away like that without telling him, and his apprenticeship hadn't even been over. That sudden escape still bothered him, pricked his conscience.

It was strange to give orders to corporals and sergeants. Something had gone, was bound to go, from their relationship, something of the old camaraderie had leaked away. Sometimes he longed with an almost physical longing to be on the square again. That mystical desire to transform men could not be experienced by these other officers. They could know nothing of it. They did not know what it meant to be a private, a non-commissioned officer. How could they possibly? They hadn't willed men to be better than they were. Some of them thought of the men as little better than scum. Hector didn't think like that.

Sometimes he felt very lonely, as if he were a stranger in a strange land, stranger even than Afghanistan. He could imagine himself a tribesman, but he was often at a loss when listening to officers' conversation about horses. They preferred horses to their men, and looked after them better. For him, however, the horse was an animal used as a beast of burden, and he had never seen dogs such as the officers talked about. They had been kind to him in the Mess but his true home was the bare windy square.

Now hands quivered in salute and voices barked out slavish words, but there was certainly a loneliness, poised between two worlds. Still, a price had to be paid and the ladder after all had towered in front of him, and he had gone over the parapet. Perhaps some day he would talk as easily about Roberts and Stewart. At the moment he was simply astonished and awed at being an officer.

However, he had better speak to the NCOs and the men about the march. He had a vague memory of a blinding snowstorm and the name Stewart. And that Afghan face twisted in hate and fear and defiance, breeding red decorations on the snow.

The march was indeed hellish. It was like walking through fire. There was no greenness to be seen anywhere, hardly any shade.

If shadows could have been made saleable, and rolled up in a commodious fashion, they would have fetched any price. Even the patch of shade under a horse girth would have been a marketable object, wrote Lieutenant Robertson later. Sand and stone everywhere and dust. And mirages which receded forever. On either side, barren mountain walls. Eternal watch must be kept against Afghans. Metal scalded the hand. Soldiers with unrecognisable dusty faces looked like devils moving eternally in that infernal fire. Horses and mules dragged themselves through a mirror-like glare.

Tantalus-like dreams of impossible draughts of ruby-coloured claret cup or amber cider used to haunt my imagination till I thought I must drink something or perish, wrote Robertson. The men, of course, were more likely to dream of beer.

And on and on they toiled as if they had become their own shadows, weightless, drifting, dreaming, for 300 miles or more, driven on by what could only be called an abstract pride in being the best force in India. The sun seemed to echo from helmets with a bronze sound. Sweat poured from them: they were dizzy with the heat. As if on the road of Empire they marched, its chosen plodding servants for ever illuminated on a secret march that would later become famous, hidden for the moment from the outside world. In blazing secrecy they sustained their pride. No one knew of them, they were lost to news and sight in that fabulous wilderness. They were a secret army turning bronze in the sun. They marched in a dream of water. Sometimes they marched by moonlight like ghosts.

But at night it was iceberg-cold. Their teeth chattered in their heads. It was often eighty degrees of temperature between the hottest point and the coldest. They were tortured by these extremes, hugging blankets to themselves at night, sweating in a prolific drench by day.

Every morning by four o'clock the army was on the march with its 1,800 animals, cows, sheep, mules and horses, and camp followers. They had ten minutes' break at the end of each hour, and twenty minutes at eight o'clock to eat, and drink coffee from their flasks. For those who sustained the long haul there was a dram at the end of the day, for the laggards who arrived late, nothing. The camp followers dropped where they were. And then the cold came down.

Dazzled, they came to Ghazni, around which there was some greenery. The pipes played, followed through the streets by a white man in Afghan clothes, dancing around them. They stared at him in amazement, as if he were a deceptive angel who had survived the fire. He pranced in front of them and around them as if from an ambiguous mirror. His dance was a mockery or a sign. His extraordinary gyrations were beyond their comprehension. They found out that his name was Dawson, that he had been stolen and raised among Afghans. He had no English except his own name which he repeated endlessly like a chant as if he wished to make himself real. He trilled innocently and happily as a child in his alien clothes. They could hardly get used to him, both enemy and friend. But they supposed anything could happen in these astounding heat-stricken mirrors.

He attached himself to them, became a servant in the Officers' Mess. He attached himself too to the pipes, to the music and colour. He followed them like an alien spirit until they returned to India, and he left them then without permission.

There too a large hunting dog attached himself to them, followed them to India, was wounded at Majuba and later died in Guernsey.

Out of the blaze of the demonic day they came at last to Kandahar after covering 300 miles in twenty days, the gates of the besieged opening in front of them. General Roberts, weak with fever, was lifted on to a horse. But the garrison was without aggressive spirit. To them the Afghans were devils who poured fire out of their nostrils. It wasn't until the relieving force came into sight that they raised the Union Jack, as if they hadn't wished to offend the Afghans, to draw their mythical ferocity upon them. That force, however, was ready to fight, to inflict on the Afghans their frustration among the delirious mirrors of the desert. Though there was some fever, most were fit, their faces burnt by the sun.

Ayub Khan's camp among the mountains was desolated by the ferocious charge of the Highland regiments and the Gurkhas and the Sikhs. His tents were captured intact. In front of Ayub Khan's tent they found the lacerated body of Lieutenant Maclean who had been captured at Maiwand. His throat had been cut. The army went berserk. It fought its way into the villages, meeting murderous fire, and into a lane enfiladed by a loopholed wall from which there poured bullets. Hector and his men thrust their guns through the walls and fired into the enclosure within. It was to be the end of the Second Afghan war, with Kandahar a climax of fire, venom and slaughter. The death of Lieutenant Maclean was pitilessly avenged on the enemy among the labyrinthine walls.

Until eventually there was silence.

Roberts was made Lord Roberts of Kandahar. His coat of arms showed a Gurkha soldier and a Gordon Highlander. Medals were also presented to Bobs' horse and to a regimental dog called Bobbie.

Hector stared implacably into that unusual silence. There was something eerie and frightening about it. In his quick climb up the ambitious peaks of Afghanistan he hadn't been confronted by this silence before. If peace came, how would he fare as an officer, whose true climate was war? Comradeship was easier in war than in peace.

Some nights the silence was so profound that he could almost hear it: there was the inevitable dissatisfaction of inaction, an emptiness waiting to be filled, an anti-climax. After the fighting what did he see in that delirious mirror? Was he in fact such an alien figure as Dawson was? Were the Kabul star which he was given and the medal struck to commemorate that famous march enough to compensate for that extraordinary dream-like campaign culminating in the final sleep-walking march which burst on the outside world like a magical revelation? And now this frightening silence. It had been almost a relief to find a real enemy waiting for them after all, to strike at real people through the mirror. Now he fell back into the exhaustion of repletion and anti-climax in a vast, seething continent almost too huge for the imagination. The sound of the bugle caused him inexpressible melancholy. He wavered as in a mirage between the sergeant he had been and the officer he was, the Kabul star nailing him to this place, the outward manifestation of that delirious confusion.

6

HECTOR was to be saved by Hamilton, who after some discussion with his fellow subalterns decided to send a telegram to Sir Evelyn Wood offering their services in the South African War which had just begun.

Not that they knew much about the intricacies of that war and the reasons for it. There was a vague idea that it was about the refusal of the Boers to pay taxes. But they didn't know anything about the Boers themselves and their hatred for the British whom they saw as an alien enemy who interfered with them continually, even replacing the Dutch language with English. They didn't know anything about the Boers' inexorable northward trek, and Natal as the lavish Eden they thirsted for. They didn't know how the Orange River sovereignty had been annexed to the Crown and how the Boer, Bible-reading and unenlightened, still thought of himself as an Old Testament prophet. They did not know about the diamonds which had been discovered by the Orange River and how the British had saved the Boers from the Zulus who were not allowed to marry until they had washed their hands in blood.

The Boers, unknown to these young officers travelling to South Africa on the 'Crocodile', had been enraged by liberal proclamations, thwarted at every step; they were an independent, suspicious race, for the most part rural in their psyche, suspicious of the city. Natives, according to them, were inferior and untrustworthy, fit only to be servants.

None of the subalterns knew anything about these hidden rancours. To Hamilton it was all a high adventure, almost schoolboyish. Macdonald of course was eager to go. He didn't want to go back to England, to loneliness. It was a God-given solution to his problem.

None of them actually thought that South Africa would be a difficult area to fight in. After all, hadn't they fought against a worse enemy, the Afghans? And the Boers were Europeans like themselves.

As the ship sailed on, they were all grateful to Hamilton who had the unconquerable fresh cheek of youth, and the security of affluence. And after that march surely they could do anything.

'They're nothing but civilians,' he would say, 'it will be a holiday. There might even be opportunities for hunting there.' They all dragged together their rags of information about South Africa, but the truth was that they didn't know much about it. They didn't think it would be as cold as Afghanistan had been or the people as treacherous. They knew vaguely that the Boers were Dutch in origin, but that didn't tell them much. Not many of them knew Dutch people. They weren't quite sure why the British were there in the first place.

And Hector himself was as ignorant as the rest of the officers, as he looked out at the blue tranquil water. He would not have been much bothered by the linguistic imperialism of English over Afrikaans, nor the same happening to Gaelic. The ironies of this odyssey escaped him. For the Boers were rural Calvinists like many of his own people, and the Old Testament was their book, not the anarchic handbooks of any revolution.

'It will be a walk-over,' said the delighted Hamilton.

'A little touch of Harry in the night,' said the ironical Robertson. Not many of the officers knew what Robertson was talking about either. They drank a toast to the Boers for giving them military employment; in fact they felt quite friendly towards them.

'As a matter of fact,' said Hamilton, 'I almost feel sorry for them. These big farm boys,' and he laughed easily. Hector didn't say anything. He was sometimes accustomed to appearing sage when he didn't know what to contribute to the conversation. There is much I might say, his appearance seemed to suggest, but I won't. The masts leaned towards the sea as they scudded along. He would sometimes stand and look over the side of the

44

ship, fascinated by the hissing white which accompanied them and also by the strange birds that appeared overhead.

God in the shape of Hamilton had been good to him. He wouldn't have to face the loneliness of a home posting just yet. He got on well with Hamilton. It was Hector who had taught him the intricacies of military evolutions on the square. Hamilton wasn't very good at that sort of thing, which in fact made him impatient and terrified of finding himself in a contortion from which he couldn't extricate himself. But there was a gaiety and an assurance in his nature which appealed to Hector and which he admired as if from a distance.

As, for instance, that insouciant telegram which Hector could never have sent himself or even have dreamed of sending.

Ah well, God worked in a mysterious way, and there was something about predestination after all.

The officers were in hysterics of laughter as they thought of farm-hands pointing guns at them like spades or forks.

Actually it wasn't like that at all. General Sir George Colley, KCST, CB, CMG had been beaten by the Boers at Laing's Nek and again at Ingoga. He was a scholar and theoretician, had passed out top of his class at Sandhurst and had written an account of the British army for the *Encyclopaedia Britannica*. He was a poet and a painter and now commander of the small army in Natal. He knew there were about 2,000 Boers camped near Laing's Nek overlooked by the volcanic hill Majuba (The Mountain of Doves). He decided to set out at night to capture the hill, and in the morning look down on the Boers from above. The Boers, commanded by the Huguenot general, Joubert, didn't think there would be an attack on a Sunday.

He took only a small part of the 92nd but mixed them with a number of inexperienced English soldiers and some men from the Naval Brigade. As they waited to leave at night, Hamilton said to Macdonald, each of them in charge of a company under the command of Major Hay, 'I can't understand climbing a mountain with all this stuff.' He watched as the men gathered together their pouches of ammunition, rations, water, blanket and trenching tool. 'I hope it's a small mountain.'

The night was fairly dark but there was a moon. One could hear cursing in the half-darkness, men cursing and muttering. Altogether there were 600 of them and twenty-two officers.

'How long does this bugger think we're going to stay at the top of this f— mountain?' Hector heard, and smiled.

Aloud he said, 'Maybe three days, maybe six.' And smiled again at the consternation of the man who had spoken.

He felt happy and cool again now that action was approaching. The first weeks as an officer had been a strain, more particularly in the Mess, though the other officers had been kind enough. But there was no question about it, he was not a social being in that sense. Shadows were struggling with their equipment in the darkness while he could see Hamilton standing slightly apart, on the edge of things.

They got the men into marching order and they were off, trying to keep as silent as possible. All that could be heard was the tramp of feet, and vague mutterings. The men were bent under their burdens as they marched into the cold night.

Eventually they saw Majuba in the half-darkness. It was higher than he had thought. The men scrambled up its steep sides, clutching at blades of grass. Sometimes a man would stumble and the others waited in silence for the sleeping Boers to waken, but nothing happened. Still the men struggled upwards, cursing, digging their boots into the sides of the mountain. It was a hard slog up these barren slopes. Still, it wasn't as high as some of the mountains in Afghanistan. Eventually they reached the top and were assigned their positions, Hector to guard a spur with about twenty men. They dug a trench at the top, around which ran a small natural parapet.

They shivered in their blankets, and then morning rose in red, and the soldiers could see the Boer camp below them. It was a peaceful Sunday morning. It was as if at any moment they might hear a cock crowing, Hector thought. A Sunday morning at home would be irreproachably quiet, just like this. All the work would have been done on the Saturday, even the dinner would have been cooked then. Men would walk to church in their severe black suits. He remembered Sunday's tremendous boredom. One was not allowed even to go for a walk, to admire God's natural works. Nature was for the rest of the week, but of course one didn't have time then.

In the rising rays the soldiers could see the camp below them. The calm was strange and eerie. The academic general, happy with his arrangements, slept on. Only the bloodshot glare troubled the Natal calm.

Then, as if terrified by the silence, desiring to break it at all costs, one of the soldiers shouted down to the Boers, 'We're here! Come up, you buggers, and fight!' Suddenly the camp below was a hive of activity. It was a sudden scurry as of ants, determined and voracious and busy. Men jumped on horseback, rifles in hands, and began to climb up the sides of the hill. The Boers could kill a deer at 400 feet from the saddle of a horse. They were protected by covering fire from the other Boers who kept the British down behind the rim of their crater.

At first General Colley was tranquil enough. What did they think they were doing? They had no hope of dislodging his army. He sent a heliograph message, 'All very comfortable. Boers wasting their ammunition. One man wounded in foot.'

Commander Romilly, commanding the Naval Brigade, wearing full staff dress, stood on the western edge and peered over the side to look at the advancing enemy. 'I say,' he said, 'there's a man who looks as if he's going to shoot at us.'

'Nine hundred yards I should say,' said his companion. A Boer bullet hit the commander in the neck, drenching his beautiful uniform with blood.

The Boers were climbing steadily and began to fire on the British soldiers who could not see the enemy. Hamilton and Macdonald waited for the order to charge, but it never came. The extinct hill had become venomous, bursting flame. It was a killing ground, blood slowly filling the crater. Shots from the British guns poured over the heads of the Boers. Colley said, 'We'll wait till they come into the open before we charge them.' The men waited as the army was systematically cut to pieces. Sniping like this was not what Colley expected from the records of the *Encyclopaedia Britannica*.

The Highlanders were growing restive, not used to being fired on without charging. Their instinct had always been to charge, to feel their bayonets in the bodies of the enemy. And now this idiot was holding them there, and they couldn't retaliate. The rays of the red sun passed over the crater. Which was the blood and which the chill red beams? The British Army began to panic. Then they began to break. General Colley, KCST, CB, CMG died from a bullet wound in the heart. He was wearing carpet slippers, footwear thought unsuitable for the men. He looked surprised, as if he had fallen asleep in his study.

Hector fought on stubbornly. Twelve of his twenty men were dead. Eight were wounded. These threw stones at the advancing Boers as they ran out of ammunition. So had Hector done once in his schooldays in mimic fight. In the carnage, as everything broke around him, he fought savagely. The Boers jumped him and tried to take his sporran, for the Boer wives used to hang them above their mantelpieces as exotic trophies. Hector kicked a big Boer in the stomach as he advanced. There was a scrummage and heavy Boers sagged on top of him. He was weeping with frustration and rage: the whole miserable episode had been mishandled. As he lay on the ground, still fighting fiercely, they took his gun, his sporran and his presentation sword (the one he had received from his fellow officers), and he was taken to the Boer camp.

He was more angry than frightened. The battle had been a bloody fiasco: not only that, but the Highlanders had panicked and broken, all because Colley would not let them charge. The Boers, however, had shown the lethal accuracy of their gunfire and a quick, deadly response to attack. Hector smiled ruefully as he remembered Hamilton's dismissive words about them. In a coldly professional way Hector admired them. In turn he was admired by the Boers who showed him an old-fashioned courtesy. Joubert offered a reward for the return of Hector's sword.

'I didn't think you would attack on a Sunday,' he said. And smiled briefly.

Hector was mentioned in despatches and promoted to full lieutenant, and the war suddenly came to an end. In the camp were young farm-hands who were marvellously deadly hunters and immensely skilful with their guns. They would flash like

48

lightning on the hills and were like Hector's own people, lovers of land, religious, flamboyant. They flashed in and out of the heavy Imperial mirror. Hector was angry with himself for having been beaten. Sometimes he had tears of rage in his eyes as he thought of what had happened, the disgrace of it. But it seemed to him that the rock had been redder where his own men had fallen.

He was released after negotiations ended in a peace, but the supposedly extinct volcano had belched out its fire, had erupted with sudden decisive force, to the shame and humiliation of the British soldiers.

Hamilton, he later found out, had, though himself wounded, rallied his men and fallen to the ground bleeding heavily. He would have been killed if an elderly Boer farmer had not intervened. He was recommended for the VC but he was considered too young, so he didn't get it.

The Gordons were taunted for their disgrace at Majuba, but Hector kept a sullen silence. The Boers had turned out after all to be more dangerous than the Afghans and far more merciful and courteous.

7

EDINBURGH, where Hector was stationed next, was also built on a volcano.

There he was confronted by the reality of his poverty and loneliness, which had been hidden before by the smoke of battle.

His fellow officers went to balls and dinners and stayed in country houses.

His own days, however, were without real purpose. In the Mess there was talk of hunts and women. Many of the officers were ignorant dummies whose uniforms blazed with history. Time lay heavy on Hector's hands, though he still played some football.

He read a great deal and walked and walked. There was much he could read about Edinburgh, about the Castle itself. The city had seen much of fighting, plagues, executions, splendid weddings, tournaments, even leprosy. There was much about witchcraft, strange diseases, strange curses.

One story left a deep impression on him. It was about a Major Weir who was a most respected figure in the city in the seventeenth century. He was very religious, a Covenanter, and he had an eloquent gift of prayer. He lived in a fine house with a private courtyard in front. In old age he was an impressive man, tall and dark: he wore a long cloak which made him appear even taller than he was: he had a stick which tapped on the cobble-stones. It seemed as if he was the perfect figure of respectability, admired, irreproachable.

One day in the year 1670 he made an announcement at one of his prayer meetings that he had committed adultery, as well as incest with his sister. Who would believe such a heroic figure?

Had his severe beliefs driven him mad? Was he lacerating his soul, his body? Had he grown tired of the dreadful weight of his uprightness; was he throwing his dignity, his honour away as if in a romantic ambiguous gesture of self-denial? Who knew what extreme belief could do to a man? Prayer meetings of course were times of confession. At times such as these one might be proud of one's sins, they were badges of the service of God. What use would one be to God without such a scarred history?

His sister, however, confirmed that the story about incest was true. She said that one night the Devil had taken her brother and herself in his blazing demonic coach with six black horses from their house to Musselburgh and back, driving at a furious speed. Now and again he would turn round and smile at them. The coach was like a fire in the night.

She said that the walking-stick had magical powers: and indeed some people then recollected that they had seen it tapping happily ahead of the major as if it had a life of its own. Bouncing merrily along the cobbled streets of old Edinburgh. The hilarity and cheerfulness of the stick!

Doctors were sent to examine the major. Was he mad, was he sane? This tall, upright figure, was he secretly laughing at them from the dangerous edge of his private precipice? Was his sister his secret malicious accomplice? This strange playfulness, where had it come from?

After examination the major was found sane. Also he was determined to pay for his sins, for those nights of the blazing coach and the six black horses, for the sunnily playful stick. On 11 April 1670 he was strangled and his stick thrown into the flames, where it burned truly enough like any other stick. His sister was hanged in the Grassmarket. The major's ghost haunted the district long after he was dead. He would ride a black horse which would vanish into flames, while he laughed uproariously. Sometimes his house was a blaze of lights, sometimes the Devil would call for him in a punctual flaming coach.

What an extraordinary story, thought Hector, consciousness of sin driving a man into loss of all that he had: house, fine possessions, outward admired respectability. Of course the stick didn't tap happily in an infernal light, like a drummer's stick, twisting and turning on its own. Of course the Devil didn't appear in a blazing coach. But the punishment was real enough.

Edinburgh was a double city, of respectability and carnality. It was famous for medicine and murder. It was a city of smelly closes, seething life, of churches and brothels, of palaces, of fine houses, violence. It was a city which echoed with the most ambiguous fictions. It had seen John Knox and Mary Queen of Scots at their embittered dialogue about two worlds – one colourful, one bleak – that would never meet except in war. Its gun, Mons Meg, had sent its huge projectiles for vast distances till it had finally exploded. It was a city of blatant class distinction. There were lawyers in it and prostitutes, beggars and lords: the squalid and formal inhabited it.

And Hector inhabited it too – for the moment a superfluous man, a poverty-stricken officer who would learn the meaning of loneliness, who must survive by continual thrift – no personal tailor for him – and present to the world as good a surface as he could manage. The ordinary soldier would happily spend his money in brothels and pubs, secure in a uniform that he didn't have to buy. Hector couldn't. He was a dummy of the Empire, stranded for the moment, hovering insubstantially about the city; without war, without battle, he was nothing. He was defined by these. He was a metaphysical conundrum, a hollow man.

So he walked about Edinburgh, in the Old Town and the New. The New was beautiful and elegant and formal, with its famous Princes Street over which the Castle loomed. There were horse-trams, shops, the gardens: in the evenings he strolled endlessly about the streets. New Edinburgh was clean and airy without the smells of the old town with its crowded slums, and its dirt and its heaving, sensual life. At the corners of the streets he saw beggars, match-sellers, women selling mussels. He even saw soldiers exhibiting wounds received at Majuba or in the Afghan war.

Old Edinburgh had tall crowded tenements. There were fist-fights, quarrels, drunken laughter. In the flaring lights he saw women garishly powdered and painted. There was an air of risk, sleazy adventure, a life on the edge of things. There was the nakedness of the human animal. Once he saw two women

52

fighting, screaming and screeching, tearing at each other's hair. There were old blind men with dogs, selling laces and pipe tops. These were the marginal people, who did not enter the shops of New Edinburgh which was spacious and handsome.

It was a city of smells, of the smell of fish, garbage, fruit, bodily odours, rotting clothes, rags. It was a city of contrasts. There were the professional classes, and the fetid, scavenging lower classes.

Once or twice he went north, to visit an aunt who stayed in Inverness-shire. She fussed about him, was proud of him, but even there he felt lonely, unsettled. His idleness depressed him. He sometimes thought about Hamilton, who maybe could have invited him to a country house, even to his own house. But he knew that he would have felt exposed, vulnerable, always looking for signals, knowing that they knew that he was not one of them. Even his uniform didn't fit him with the dapper sleekness that could be seen in the uniform of those officers – all of them, really – who could afford personal tailors.

While his aunt chattered on and asked about his experiences, he knew that he couldn't really tell her what it had been like. Even now it was sometimes like a dream. What was India to this place in Inverness-shire, what was Africa to it? He liked his aunt, but she wasn't someone he could really talk to. Her life had been happy, cheerful, but limited. She was proud when he went to church with her on a Sunday. She wished to show him off. And he indulged her. But it was as if he was looking for some reward – was that it? – for those fighting days and nights. And all that had come out of them was this silence, this idleness.

He would go for long walks, admiring the landscape, its summer or autumnal beauty. There were heathery moors, rivers, lochs. It was all very peaceful, serene, as his aunt was. Trees reflected themselves with absolute fidelity in the water, rowans blazed with their red wounds. He was neither happy here nor in Edinburgh. He wondered whether he would be happy anywhere.

*

One evening in Edinburgh he watched an open-air concert in Princes Street Gardens, and began to speak to a fifteen-year-old girl, whose name he later found out was Christine Duncan. He was thirty years old: she appeared young, virginal, pure, and she loved military music. It was a lyrical moment for Hector, it flowered out of his loneliness. It was not uncommon for there to be such an age difference in lovers. Men had experience of the world, women not. Women were divided into the pure and the impure. The impure lived in the tenements, Christine lived in Frederick Street. Hector was lonely, the event was inevitable or seemingly so.

The meeting is easily imaginable. Loneliness can be very tiring, filled with bodiless images. Then into a particular space there comes a real living being, young, vibrant, hopeful. A real presence of a kind is instantly sketched out, with solidity and warmth. There is somebody waiting for one in a world which is otherwise a fantasy with equally indifferent pictures around one. The blood, the violence are forgotten. The world is not composed wholly of these. Nor simply of order, it is lyrical order with its own unexpectednesses.

It is important to remember this, for later Hector did not see much of Christine. He had a child by her, but he did not even correspond with her much. It was an affair which arose out of loneliness and perhaps the military music. He was wearing civilian clothes, which did not fit him properly. Once or twice he had to ask his brother William for money, which he did not like doing. There was a gaucheness about him, an innocence which attracted her.

At any rate it was she who, caught up in her vivid, excited world, said to him, 'It is so beautiful' (meaning the music).

'Isn't it?' he said. He tried to think of something else to say and eventually managed, 'Do you like this kind of music?'

'Oh, I do, I do.'

She looked at him, imagined him quite clearly as a soldier, even though he was in civilian clothes. She saw him on the glamorous fields of Empire, she confided to him suddenly, 'I know you are a soldier. We are told about the Empire in school. I would like to go to India.'

For a moment Hector thinks of India. It seems very far away. He remembers the bodies dangling from ropes, the stinking dead camels, a dead icy eye. It's almost as if he had never been there, as if he had just read about it. He's forgotten many of the names of the places.

'It's very big,' he says. He makes an effort. 'Very big and mountainous.'

'I know that,' she says. 'But it's much more than that. The caravans, the temples, the clothes. The mystery of it.'

And then, as if she had suddenly heard him, 'Did you serve there?'

'Yes.'

'Did you see the temples? In school all they talk about is latitude and longitude, products.' She imitates the teacher. 'Among other things India is famous for ivory.'

'We didn't have much time. We were mostly in Afghanistan.'

'Did you not see elephants then?'

'Yes.'

'And they say the women are very beautiful. And the dresses.'

She looked at him keenly. With her ancient woman's wisdom she was asking him, Did you go out with some of these women?

But some of the women he had seen in Afghanistan hadn't been like that at all. They were said to have knives in their hands or hidden in their clothes.

He did not want her to know about the blood. Better let her stay among her latitudes and longitudes. But she did not stay there.

Now she was playful and teasing. He was like a big solid heavy bull around which she waved her vivid red flag.

'Why, I would have seen more myself,' she said. 'I'm not sure if you were there at all. But of course men don't notice much. I would have noticed everything.'

He found out that she stayed in Frederick Street and that her father was a teacher.

'He isn't as interested in geography as I am,' said Christine.

She was of course respectable. Their house would be comfortable. He imagined her father for a moment on the analogy of Mr Treasurer, but then thought that he would probably be more formidable. He couldn't imagine Mr Treasurer in a school in Edinburgh.

'My father doesn't like me going out on my own,' she said. 'But of course it's only a short distance. And I'm old enough.' She tosses her hair back in an instinctive female gesture.

He stood at last on her doorstep. He didn't wish to leave, to return to the barracks. What had he to return to? He was confused by a strange feeling of protectiveness for her, for her vivid innocence, as if she were a sister, and yet at the same time he felt that she was more worldly than he.

'I shall invite you to supper,' she said as they parted. 'It will be easier as you are an officer. My father does what I tell him anyway,' she said as she disappeared. He waited there for a while after she had gone.

It was as if she was a vision, as if she didn't exist. And yet, after all, didn't Edinburgh itself look like a theatre with its fairy-tale castle, where he was in fact stationed? She was well off, she was completing her education. Her family belonged originally to Perth. All this she had told him in her quick, vivid manner. He was a lieutenant, he had no money, she was very young. He turned away from the door. Two young women in bright finery smiled at him as they walked past: he smelt their perfume. But he was absorbed in innocence, in girlishness. On the other hand he felt rather frightened. He had had few dealings with women or girls. What responsibilities, if any, was he taking on, especially if he met her family?

The meeting seemed unreal and yet at the same time it had arisen out of his loneliness. He had never felt, for instance, as if he should get married, even if the rules had allowed it. Wasn't that odd? Sometimes of course he had felt sexual urges, but had studied and kept them at bay. Also he had played football. But here he was very lonely and his life lacked direction.

Thinking these thoughts, he made his way back to the Castle.

*

56

In fact in later days he became a rather comic figure. He met Christine outside her school and carried her books for her. He waited there obediently, impatiently, till he saw her coming, distinguishing her quickly from all the others, and taking the books from her. She had her chattering secret female school friends. Did they not envy her this strong-looking upright man waiting for her? Of course they did, and of course she told them that he was an officer, that he had served in Afghanistan, India, South Africa.

She felt herself much superior to them, even to the teacher who taught them geography. After all, he hadn't been to Afghanistan. She could tell him stories if she wanted to. And the same with India and South Africa. For her the latitudes and longitudes and temperatures were transformed by colour.

She did not need to learn her femininity, it was instinctive. This was a man who commanded men and she commanded him. Of course she did not think like this abstractly, but that was what she did. She waved to her friends and walked slowly to meet him, to prolong the moment. She felt their envious gazes on her back. She demonstrated her worldly carelessness to them and was delighted when he looked impatient, though that happened seldom. She hoped the other girls were watching: they must be writhing with jealousy.

She said to him as they walked along, 'Do you find the books heavy?' (Laughing delightedly to herself at the notion. But he really did look rather comic, as if he hadn't handled books for a long time.)

'Of course not.'

'What school did you attend yourself?' (Skipping along beside him and turning to look at him.)

'It was a small country school. Very small.' He couldn't bring himself to tell her about that thatched roof, the rain that sometimes came in, the peat for the fire.

'Did you like it?'

'It was all right.'

'I bet you were very clever.'

'Not so clever as all that.'

'Did you play tricks on the teacher?'

'We did.'

'We sometimes do on ours. Judith stares at him longingly as if she is swooning. It embarrasses him.' (And she laughs loudly.)

'And you fought, I suppose,' she said.

'Yes. After school. We'd make up teams and throw stones at each other.'

'How barbaric.'

He pondered this for a while as he strode along.

'I suppose we must have been,' he admitted at last. He had even heard of pupils who had hidden behind peat banks and thrown stones at the teacher. But that was fun, Mr Treasurer wasn't really unpopular.

She liked his soft Highland accent: it was gentle and pleasant. In fact he always gave an impression of gentleness, which was odd since he had been in wars. She supposed that was how soldiers must be, laconic, not at all garrulous. But she wished that he would talk more.

'Sometimes,' she said, 'you are like an officer I have seen in a book.' She examined him. He suffered her examination patiently. He was in fact hers, she could hardly believe it. And he was always correct, neat, though his suit didn't exactly fit him.

'It's so funny to see you carrying my books as if they were crockery that would break if you dropped them. After all, they're only silly old Euclid and grammar.'

He smiled. He was always good-tempered. He had natural good manners, though he didn't bow or scrape. She would hate him to do that.

'What did your father do?'

'He was a stone-mason. I used to travel about with him.'

'Was it nice?'

'No, it wasn't nice.'

(To find a byre to sleep in. It was all right in the summer. But in the winter it hadn't been nice.)

'I think you're very calm,' she would say to him.

'Oh?'

'That's why I like to talk to you. You're a strong, silent man. You've seen so much and you're so calm. I bet if a horse got out of control and came at us you would remain calm.'

'I don't know about that,' he said, 'but I would do my best.'

Once she asked him quietly, 'Did you ever kill anyone?' Her voice was very low and she looked at him intently. He had never thought that she would ask him this question.

'Yes,' he said.

'In hand-to-hand combat? With swords and sabres?'

'Yes.'

She let her mind rest on that image. It was sparkling and adventurous, a picture in a book. It was not in any way clouded by real blood.

But all this was after the supper party.

Christine had done her job well, for both parents were friendly.

'So you're the young man my daughter has told me about,' said the father. Hector sat upright in the chair almost as if he were sitting at attention. The mother smiled at him and asked him to take some sweet, which, however, was rather heavy for Hector.

At one point the father said, 'So you've been fighting abroad?'

'Yes, indeed,' said Christine. 'He's been to India and South Africa.'

'What did you think of the Boers?' said her father.

'Good soldiers, sir. Unorthodox. They beat us at Majuba.' (The memory of Majuba returned like a sharp wound. Even now fights could be caused in pubs by soldiers from other regiments taunting the Gordons.)

'So you were at Majuba?'

'I'm afraid so, sir.'

'It wasn't his fault, Father, that we got beaten. He wasn't the commanding officer.'

'I see you're his advocate,' said her father, smiling affectionately. 'It surprised us at home.'

'It surprised us too,' said Hector. It had been his first touch of humour and it surprised even himself for he wasn't a witty man.

'I understand you rose from private.'

'Indeed he did, Papa.'

(The mother thought that it would have been too much to hope for a son-in-law who was what she called an officer of family. Still, the boy must have character and that was important too. Though of course he could hardly be called a boy any more.)

59

'Of course, Christine, that is exactly what I was saying,' said her father. But it was perhaps not what he was saying. Yet Hector gave an impression of quiet strength as one who had suffered and acted. He made the imaginative leap towards the mountains of Afghanistan or the bloody rock of Majuba. Hector was an exotic though soberly plumaged bird in their room.

They played whist, and Hector felt the warm atmosphere of the family. It was a long time since he had felt such security, such female consideration. The mother was the best strategist of all at cards. Hector wasn't used to playing cards. He never took part in gambling, partly because he didn't have any money and partly because he had an instinctive antipathy to it, perhaps as a result of his religious upbringing.

At one point in the conversation, while gathering in a number of 'tricks', the mother said casually, 'Of course I understand that the Gordons have a regulation that marriage is out of the question till the rank of captain is reached.'

'That is so, ma'am,' said Hector.

(Now how did she find that out, thought the father wonderingly. But women often amazed him. Their knowledge was simply different from his own.)

'Ha, I make diamonds trumps,' said the mother imperiously.

No, I can't imagine marriage, thought Hector. I don't know how it is, but I simply cannot imagine it. I am used to order, to the abstract regularity of drill, and so I cannot imagine disorder. He instinctively sensed that marriage would bring disorder into his life.

And yet what about this monastic loneliness? Could he endure that? He was on the horns of a dilemma, loneliness or a marriage that would disturb his sense of order.

The mother was saying, 'You will be quite lonely, I suppose. I mean, in peacetime there can't be much for a soldier to do. Especially when he is in barracks.'

'It is not so exciting as war,' said Hector.

'I'm sure it isn't,' said Christine, her eyes shining, thinking of brilliant swords.

The father drew the conversation away to more masculine subject matter. 'You've seen General Roberts, I take it?'

'Yes, sir, he commanded us in Afghanistan. The men would follow him anywhere. They call him Old Bobs.'

'I've read about him. He seems very competent. That march of his . . . we were all on tenterhooks.'

'Hector saw the temples and the elephants and he even guarded the Prince of Wales,' said Christine eagerly. 'He guarded him when he was in India. He stood outside his tent. Isn't that right, Hector?'

'Yes,' said Hector shyly.

'I have read of India,' said her father consideringly. 'Their religion is different from ours. Also, their sense of time.' He spoke in his teacher's voice as if he was passing judgment on a whole civilisation. 'They do not understand our Western energy.'

It bothered him momentarily that Hector had seen so much of the world, that his daughter obviously and flagrantly admired the glamorous adventurer, though he did not really look glamorous in his civvies. He was not exactly the kind of person that he had foreseen for his daughter. An Othello to her Desdemona, enchanting her with his strange stories, though on the other hand it must be admitted that he wasn't grandiloquent. Still, he had fought hand-to-hand with desperate tribesmen. That must change a man. That must make him different. He wasn't a good card player, though. His wife was far more astute. Still, that was a good thing, it meant that he wasn't a gambler.

Christine saw war as dramatic and exciting: for him it was more than that – eerie, unimaginable, the charge with the bayonet, the hand-to-hand fights. And yet this young man looked quite ordinary, embarrassed, as if not used to company. A man of the camp indeed. According to Christine he had run away from home to join the army. He was obviously dedicated, perhaps even obsessive. He glanced at his daughter. He said silently to her, No, my dear, I could not have done what this young man has done. On the contrary, I am happy with talk, not action. He wondered whether any good would come of this: reality was more important than glamour and glamour itself was the light cast by ignorance. Perhaps to some people his own teaching might appear glamorous. This soldier entering the domestic world was foreign and ultimately unintelligible. How much of himself would he be able to give? Christine was young and had the instinctive cunning of women. She could manipulate him perhaps easily enough. And there was her mother to support her.

The domestic silence throbbed with a strange presence. Christine's mother coughed gently as she won a trick. The cards glittered on the table. Kings and queens, colourful and imperial. Hector's hands moved clumsily among them.

8

SOMETIMES, even after he had been seeing Christine, Hector felt that his relationship with her was odd, that even if marriage were possible, it was unreal. It was hard to express even to himself what he felt. It was perhaps something to do with the army, his love of the absolute and formal, as if Christine would be a barrier to the attainment of that perfection. It was not a place for women, that arena, he felt obscurely. Women, he felt, would not be able to understand.

At times Christine would talk as if they were already married, and sitting in a house which she had already chosen and whose furniture she had selected. There would also be a garden, for she was fond of flowers. Hector could not imagine such a house and himself as head of it. Sometimes she would say to him, in a sudden excess of affection, 'Would you like red curtains on the windows? Lots of people have heavy red velvet curtains.'

But he couldn't imagine such a house nor the two of them in it. It wasn't that he wasn't fond of her. What he wanted was for the two of them to meet each other without marriage being mentioned. Should he therefore stop seeing her? Was that not the honourable thing to do? But on the other hand not seeing her was also unimaginable: he couldn't bear a return to his loneliness. Not to see her, not to take joy in her vivid certainty was not possible for him. For she had a deeper hope in the world than he had and this, he realised, was part of her womanly nature. The army had fixed him in a structure but it was a structure that had nothing to do with the real universal world. It was an artificial structure that belonged to the army alone.

In her presence he would often forget his perplexity. She was so quick. She noticed far more than he did. If they were walking in a park she would be the first to see a squirrel or rabbit. She was infinitely aware of the world. Compared with her he was a blind man. She would pass a woman on the street and say, 'Imagine wearing brown and purple together.'

She would stop for a long time looking at rings in jewellers' shops. She loved all kinds of jewellery, not perhaps because she was greedy but because she liked glittering things. She had a great deal of knowledge of precious stones. In his world, even in his early world, jewellery didn't figure greatly. His mother had her plain wedding ring, that was all.

One day, she would say to him, 'We can afford to go into a jeweller's.' She would clutch spontaneously at his arm, so that he trembled with the overpowering grace of it.

He had always to remember that she was young, much younger than he was, and that what she had seen of the world was different. She was not yet aware of the limits set by adulthood; she had a fragrance of optimism.

'I don't understand why they have that rule in the Gordons,' she would say. 'It's such a stupid rule. After all, I would like to go with you to see the world. I'm not afraid of discomfort. And in any case I wouldn't interfere with your work. I would go to the shops in Delhi, there's so much that I want to see.' And she would clap her hands excitedly. After all, they were alive only once: why shouldn't they make the most of it? When she said that she wouldn't interfere with his work, she didn't realise that it was not deliberate intrusion on her part that would do that, it was her very presence, the alternative that she presented.

Joy bubbled in her continually. Once at the seaside she hurled stones across the surface of the water, delighting in their smooth, exhilarating rush. 'You do it too,' she said. And Hector did it as well. She marvelled at the speed of the stones but she wasn't interested in scientific explanations.

'Don't be so stiff and sober,' she would say to him, pulling at his moustache. 'I would like to travel on a great big liner. The sea is so mysterious. I don't think there is anything as mysterious as the sea. But I don't think I would be seasick. We are reading a poem about an albatross. I like it.'

Another time she would say, 'I would like you to teach me mathematics. I can't understand it, especially algebra. I can't follow all that stuff about Xs and Ys. I don't know what they mean. I much prefer art to mathematics.'

Sometimes, as if trying to be superior to him, she would speak a few words of French, and he would answer in Gaelic or even Urdu.

'You are quite a linguist,' she would say. 'Tell me what is "sweetheart" in Gaelic.' And he would say awkwardly 'leannan', and she would try to repeat the word after him. 'Tell me my name in Gaelic,' and he would say 'Carstiona'.

Her changes were dazzling. At times she was a young girl and would talk like one, sometimes in school slang. At times, assuming the future, she would talk in a mature way, very seriously. These changes often confused him. It was as if he wanted the world to be mathematical, conforming to a central idea. She had no central idea. That was why she saw the squirrel first in the park, for she devoured the world as it was. Sometimes for no apparent reason – and this puzzled him – she would burst into tears, and if he asked her what was wrong she would say impatiently, 'Leave me alone, leave me alone. Don't cross-examine me.'

What indeed were these tears for? At last he grew to accept them and would remain silent even when she was crying. He saw them as an ultimate mystery for ever closed to him.

With regard to Edinburgh itself, he liked it. There was at times an open, breezy feeling to the city which invigorated him, so that he would step out as if he were marching in a transparent air. Christine would dance along beside him.

Nevertheless he was idling: in some sense he was not doing what he should be doing, and this bothered him. A soldier in peacetime was a paradox. He might have his drill and his administration, but on the other hand he wasn't acting in the real military world, he wasn't being tested by the realities of war, he was learning nothing new. He felt this idleness as a gap at the centre of his being. He felt it was indecent. He was like a violinist who wasn't playing the violin, a pianist who couldn't play the piano.

He felt guilty, for he had been brought up in a world where

work was important, was a manifestation of the task laid by God on man after he had rebelled. A man was defined by work, was sometimes known by his work.

In a sense this romantic interlude with Christine was a waste of time. It wasn't real. It wasn't where his deepest reality was. For even as he walked the streets he saw busy people, bakers, butchers, carriers, drapers. They were involved in what they had chosen.

He, on the contrary, was always waiting. What he had to do hadn't yet arrived, and wasn't even on the horizon. But he was waiting for it. And not even the presence of Christine could assuage that feeling of the future.

One night Christine's father told him the story of Deacon Brodie who had been a respectable councillor by day and a robber by night. He had eventually escaped to Holland but had been brought back to Edinburgh to be hanged.

'I can't understand why he did it. Surely it can't have been for the money?' Hector could have told him why. Obviously it wasn't for the money: on the contrary, it was for the excitement, for those nights when he had lived at the tips of his senses, when he had watched the shadows for his pursuers. He had been tired of the fixed reality of his councillor's life.

'He is supposed to have liked *The Beggar's Opera*,' said Mr Duncan. Hector knew nothing of *The Beggar's Opera* and Mr Duncan explained it to him. 'Even at the end Brodie was quite calm,' he said. 'He had a plan for escape. He would bribe the hangman to shorten the rope and then he would be rushed to a doctor. So he was quite calm at the scaffold. But in fact this could not be done – I imagine the hangman was carefully watched or maybe the plot was revealed – and so he died.'

Hector could see exactly why Brodie had done what he had done, but he couldn't explain it to the conventional Mr Duncan. For Brodie the night would have glittered with adventure, passions, with plans and plots hostile to bourgeois Edinburgh. He would have had similar feelings to Hector when in battle he lived on the tips of his senses. All these adventures showed the precariousness of life, oblique and glistening. As he set off in his duplicitous cloak and false wig, Brodie was tasting life on his tongue. He might even have been a good soldier in different

66

circumstances, spawning tactics from his fresh brain. Hector himself had always noticed that the best soldiers were those with a touch of the devil in them, the almost untameable ones. Many had been thieves or rascals, for whom risk and battle were ideal. So he could understand Brodie, whose neck was broken; whose body was given to two workers from the Brodie yard, who placed it in a cart and drove furiously down the steep slope of the Netherbow, then round the cobbles of the Grassmarket, where the French quack was waiting with his lancet ready. But it was too late.

And Brodie was dead and buried quietly in the churchyard near George Square.

Once Mrs Duncan took Hector aside and asked him frankly about his intentions towards her daughter. She looked suddenly firm and serious.

'She is very young,' she said.

She questioned him about his prospects, his income. She was not impressed. Hector felt like a schoolboy in front of her. This materialistic interrogation embarrassed him. It made his careless outings with Christine seem strangely soiled.

'However, you are a man of good conduct and Christine likes you, though it is a pity that because of military regulations you are not a more senior officer. Then there would be no problem.'

She paused, and then said, 'I hear that your regiment will soon be leaving Edinburgh. Is that correct?'

(How had she found out about that? thought Hector. Mothers of young daughters seemed to have sources of information which could not be fathomed.)

'Yes, ma'am,' said Hector.

'In that case then,' she said, 'it might be as well if you plighted your troth. This can take place in the house. It is not so satisfactory as a proper marriage but it can be confirmed and ratified later. Is that agreeable to you?'

'Yes, ma'am.'

She looked at him intently and sighed.

'You are a strange fellow at times. It is as if you were not there at all, as if you were merely agreeing to my suggestions without thinking. But you must understand, Christine is young. If I do not look after her, who will? I hope Christine will not find you as absent as I sometimes do.'

The large opulent Victorian furniture was reflected in the mirror. Hector felt constricted as if he could not breathe. He found himself staring into that distant reflected room as if, unlike the real one, it could confer freedom on him. Surely when he had first met Christine he had not imagined this business-like confrontation? He had been manoeuvred into a narrow space by a clever general, or so it seemed to him.

Mrs Duncan looked suddenly larger, more commanding than she had seemed before. He wondered if Christine knew what was happening. Perhaps she did. In another situation he would have hacked his way out with his sword, but here he was silent, dumbfounded. Mrs Duncan seemed much more worldly-wise than he, more certain of the conventions by which her life was ruled. And yet he could understand her concern. It was just that everything had suddenly become very blunt. His Highland sensibilities, shy and almost demure, were offended.

'Are you all right, Hector?'

'Yes, ma'am, perfectly all right.'

She sighed again and said, 'I hope you realise that marriage has serious responsibilities, though it also brings joys. It is the natural situation for adults to be in. Christine has been well brought up and we expect her to lead a comfortable life. At the moment she has certain romantic notions but these will diminish as she grows older. She will depend on you: I hope you realise that.'

The chairs and table were solid in that reflected light. On the wall there was a sombre landscape possibly of somewhere in Perthshire. It showed a torrent of water pouring down a rock. In the middle of the water there seemed to be boulders.

'And now we will bring Christine in,' said Mrs Duncan. 'Afterwards we will have coffee.'

*

Just before he left for the Sudan, a country about which he knew nothing, Hector was walking down Leith Walk with Christine. It was a lovely calm day: Edinburgh appeared at its best: formal, busy, historical. They saw old blind fiddlers at corners. Sailors strolled along the street. There were cripples in vehicles drawn by dogs.

Christine was not happy: he, however, was filled with purpose as a ship by a sudden unexpected wind. She sensed this, as she sensed everything, as she watched the sailors in their blue uniforms.

'Are you happy to be going?' she said to him.

'I would be if I were not leaving you,' he answered diplomatically.

'I can tell you are happy,' she said.

A sailor was rolling along singing a ballad. She clasped Hector's hand in hers as if she did not wish to let go of him. She was very pale. He felt sorry because he was so happy, because he felt purpose returning to him. Sudan too would be another country which he had not seen. It would probably be as hot as India.

But he felt almost a certain impatience with her, as if she were holding him back.

'I wish I could come with you,' she said. 'I looked up the Sudan. It is very hot there. Also, there is not much vegetation.'

'Maybe some day you will come with me,' he said tactfully.

There was a slight breeze blowing along the street. It whirled some dust with it. There was a butcher in a striped smock standing at the door of a shop. His stripes were white and blue and he was absently holding a cleaver in his hand. The naked body of a sheep hung on a hook.

Christine felt the freshness of the breeze as a threat. It reminded her of new worlds and new partings.

'You will write to me?' she said.

'Of course.'

His eyes were on the blind beggar at the corner. He reminded him of the day he had left the shop in Inverness entirely impulsively. But he had no money to give the beggar and this troubled him. This was a man destroyed in the service of his country. The bill which proclaimed this was like a shield or a gravestone. Not so long ago he himself had been defeated at Majuba. He remembered quite clearly being given back his sword, but at the same time the memory of the defeat still rankled.

'Do you like my mother?' said Christine suddenly.

'Yes,' said Hector.

Her mother had talked of his being a captain or a major. In a way he had found this distasteful, embarrassing. It had nothing to do with what he felt about Christine whom he placed on a pedestal in his mind, virginal, untainted. But he wished sometimes she would talk less, question him less. He had been so used to camp that he didn't like talking.

'I know you resent her,' said Christine.

It was as if she was looking for a quarrel with him, for she knew with her feminine intuition that he was glad to be going, that he felt unchained. For a moment she regretted the army as well, wished that he did some other job, saw the army as her enemy. At times like these he found her emotional, puzzling. Her world bore no relation to the world of the army with its exact arrangements, its inflexibility, its impersonality. At times her world was one of wet handkerchiefs. She would read something from the newspaper and cry. His world was different; it was conducted for the most part in the open air. His life had been one in the open air. Hers had big furniture in it, thoughts about houses. Christine was not free from the weakness of her kind, and yet she had helped him. Did he love her? He wasn't sure what that meant.

'I must be going back,' he said. 'I still have much to do.'

'If I could go with you I would be happy,' she said. She liked touching him. 'You never say "I love you",' she would say to him. 'I have to say it all the time.' But his mind was settling on the Sudan, hovering over it, thinking what he would be doing there. In his military abilities he wasn't mistaken. He was only uneasy in this feminine world which was as unfathomable to him as the Sudan was at that moment.

She kissed him as they parted. She shivered for a moment as if she was saying goodbye to him. Before he could say anything she had run away from him and didn't look back. Perhaps he should run after her, perhaps that was required of him. But he

70

didn't do that. He turned away in the direction of the Castle which crouched over Princes Street like a pyramid.

Three years after Hector had left Edinburgh and while he was back on leave, Christine conceived a child by him.

Only much later, in 1894, the 'plighting of their troth' (a marriage in the old Scots style) was declared legal when Christine appeared before the Court of Session. She said that Hector had 'visited constantly at her father's house, paid her marked attention, and made professions of love to her'. She agreed to marriage taking place between them by exchanging consents. He had taken a Bible and asked her to swear. She had said, 'I solemnly swear and declare that I take you, Hector Macdonald, to be my husband, to love, honour and obey, so help me God.' He took her as his wife. They had both kissed the book. He made her promise that she would not reveal the marriage.

And that was that.

9

HAMILTON was very angry. 'So that's it,' he said, 'Gordon's dead and the march was futile.'

'Perhaps it was his own fault,' said Robertson, looking out at the Nile.

'What do you mean by that?' said Hamilton.

'He was given his chance to come out time after time,' said Robertson. 'You know that. Maybe he wanted to be a hero, a martyr.'

'I think that's a disgraceful thing to say,' said Hamilton. 'What do you think, Mac?'

'I think,' said Hector slowly, 'that the Dervishes should be punished.'

'We haven't got a proper army yet,' said Robertson. 'And in any case Wilson was useless. He waited for days after they had crossed the desert. He should have gone straight to Khartoum.'

'Another Colley,' said Hamilton scornfully. 'Another civil servant.'

'Mind you,' said Hector calmly, 'his army would have been exhausted.'

'They waited too long,' said Hamilton scornfully. 'Of course they did. The days they waited were absolutely crucial.'

'I still think it was Gordon's own fault,' said Robertson, beating at a fly that was encircling his neck. 'He could have come out long ago. He was a strange fellow, anyway. I've heard he was very religious and odd. Do you know that he once said he found the Garden of Eden in the Seychelles? My own feeling deep down is that he wanted to be a martyr.'

'You mean he wanted his head chopped off by the Mahdi,'

72

said Hamilton mockingly. 'I wouldn't have thought any sane man would have wanted that.'

'Look,' said Robertson, equally mockingly, 'why do you think we're here, anyway? It's all a question of economics. Britain wants to keep control over the Suez Canal. It's as simple as that. And now what will we do?'

The heat beat down on them but the Nile looked tranquil.

'And another thing,' said Robertson, 'this war has been fought on the cheap. I think the Mahdi has better weapons than us.'

'They say,' said Hector, 'that the Dervishes are good fighters.'

'Yes, they believe that if they die they will go straight to heaven,' said Robertson. 'So they don't mind dying. And I still maintain that Gordon could have come out earlier. The fact is, however, that he will have to be revenged. It may take time but the Mahdi can't be allowed to get away with his murder. That is the way things go.'

'And I know the very man to do it,' said Hamilton enthusiastically. 'Kitchener.'

'Another odd fellow,' said Robertson.

'Yes, but very brave,' said Hamilton. 'Do you know that he was a spy in the desert? Apparently he carried a phial of poison in his head-dress to swallow if he was caught. Naturally he would have been tortured. One shudders at the kind of death he might have died.'

'Oh, he's brave, no one's saying he isn't,' said Robertson. 'But he's a bit like Gordon himself. A loner. All bachelors are odd, like Mac here. Kitchener loves china and flowers for example. And he's a sort of Hamlet. They say he doesn't have much conversation.'

'Nothing disguises the fact that it's another defeat,' said Hamilton. 'Like Majuba. Too late, too late. And all Wilson's fault.'

'Well,' said Hector calmly, 'they would have had a long march. They would have to fight for the wells. And apparently they were sold old camels. Then a lot of them had boils from the flies. They were exhausted.'

'I would have made for Khartoum,' said Hamilton angrily. 'He dithered and dithered. All these civil servants are the same.'

'His commanding officer died on him,' said Hector equably. 'He had no experience of high command.'

'Then he shouldn't have been there,' said Hamilton. 'Bloody flies,' and he brushed one away.

All around them bronzed men were hauling at ammunition boxes.

'So now we go back with our tails between our legs,' said Hamilton. 'I'm so angry about it.'

'The trouble is,' said Robertson, 'that there are thousands and thousands of Dervishes. And they'll all be cock-a-hoop now. We'll need a lot of preparations before we take them on, if we take them on at all.'

'Kitchener will take them on,' said Hamilton confidently. 'I'm sure of that. Do you know that Gordon wanted him to be Governor of the Sudan? Gordon was a dreamer. I agree as far as that with you,' he said, turning to Robertson.

'I bet he went to meet them like a bridegroom,' said Robertson. 'I'm sure he wanted his death. It is such a beautiful legend. It is better to have commanding officers who don't want to die. What do you think, Mac?'

'Mac certainly doesn't want to die,' said Hamilton, laughing. 'Look at him. Bronzed and strong. I'm sure he doesn't want to die, though he's a Celt. And I don't want to die. Life is beautiful except for these bloody flies.'

'I'm serious,' said Robertson. 'We want commanding officers who are slightly stupid. No, stupid is the wrong word, ambitious ones who want to get to the very top. Egotists.'

'They say Kitchener is like that,' said Hamilton. 'They say he is very ambitious.'

'Good for him,' said Robertson. 'Let him want to live to be a general.' And he thought of Gordon. He had a picture of a bachelor who had waited till the inevitable happened, who had wished to die, and had walked out to be killed. With a dramatic sense of timing. No, that wasn't the way to be a general. Old Bobs' way was the best, to actively enjoy being a general, to want to win. He looked out at the Nile, which seemed pretty but had a lot of crocodiles in it. Poor Gordon, just the same. His death must have been a hard one. The skull rotting somewhere now. And he suddenly felt as angry as Hamilton.

This bloody desert, these bloody flies. It was hotter than South Africa, in its own way hotter than the march to Kandahar. The sand got into your boots, into your eyes, when there was one of these whirlwinds. Into the food. It was not a country for civilised fighting, and he smiled, though Mac looked happy enough. He brushed another large fly away from him. Christ knew what diseases were waiting, malaria for one.

Hamilton had sat down on an ammunition box. Hector was still standing. The sun blazed down, and Robertson wiped his face. This bloody country. All the bloody hauling they had had to do. Boats, equipment. There must be a better way than this. And the men's boots were inadequate. He kicked irritably at a stone and saw an insect running away. Perhaps a lizard.

'It's the government at home,' said Hamilton. 'They didn't care. They let Gordon die. It's as simple as that. They want an Empire but they want it on a shoestring.'

'Maybe some of them don't want it at all,' said Robertson. 'But I agree with you. You can't fight a war on the cheap. On the other hand religion can be very powerful. The Mahdi seems to have convinced his followers of their destiny. He must be an extraordinary man in his own way. So of course was Gordon.'

'I believe he was very religious too,' said Hamilton.

'His religion was not much use to him here,' said Robertson. 'Religion needs modern fire power if it is going to survive. That is what we must have.'

His eyes glinted delightedly as they always did when he had produced an epigram. And yet there was a certain truth in what he had just said. Not even religion could survive without gunnery, and gunnery had to be executed properly. The trouble was that the Mahdi had been allowed to make the running. He had read somewhere that when Gordon was at Gravesend where he had served as an engineer, he would give out religious tracts, running alongside trains to hand them out, hopping along in his absorbed, scholarly manner. On leave he had walked about Jerusalem looking for the exact spot where Christ had been crucified. But the British soldier was not about to rush on the enemy to find his heaven. On the other hand, if he had good guns he didn't have to. The trouble was that at the moment he didn't even have good guns.

'What do you think about that?' he asked Hector suddenly.

'What?' Hector seemed to emerge out of a private dream.

'That good guns will defeat a religion.'

'Oh, that's true,' said Hector, 'it happened in the Highlands too.' It had happened at Culloden when good military preparations had stopped the wild rushes of the Highlanders. Yes, what Robertson said was true, no question about it. But did the Dervishes have what could be called a good religion? His Scottish conscience felt that in fact they didn't, and that they were savages. It wasn't heaven that was waiting for them but hell. And in any case after this heat they wouldn't feel the difference. He smiled to himself. Sometimes he had thoughts like these but didn't find it as easy as Robertson to voice them.

He was more worried about what would happen to him next now that Gordon's death had brought the war to an end. He didn't wish to return to Britain nor to a peacetime station. After Edinburgh the climate was certainly hot, but on the other hand he didn't wish that period of boredom again. Sometimes, however, he felt guilty about Christine. On the march he had forgotten about her. No one of course knew that he was married to her. He seemed another of the eternal bachelors of his time, like Gordon, like Kitchener. Of course Kitchener didn't like his officers to be married. He believed that marriage took away from their military dedication, and possibly from their dedication to himself. But it bothered Hector that Christine had become part of the civilian world, distant, misty, almost unreal. More real were the Nile, the big flies, the movement about him of soldiers, the blue sky, the snickering of horses, the boats, Hamilton sitting like a statue on his box, and the eternal satirical and knowledgeable Robertson.

And another defeat.

Sometimes in fact he would sit down and try to write to Christine. But he wasn't sure that what he could say interested her. And there was a certain monotony about war too, which civilians didn't understand. How far was she interested in the details of the march? In the lifting of these boats over cataracts? In the actual

76

details? And as for her own letters, they were monotonous too, with their talk about Edinburgh, which seemed to him so far away. It was as if he had made a mistake, an error which had arisen from his loneliness. How else could he explain the unreality of his marriage? The marriages of the men in his company were more real to him, he was sure.

And yet he had this guilt all the time. Well, perhaps not all the time, but a good deal of the time. He looked out at the Nile. It seemed so calm, yet perhaps it wasn't really. He put his hand briefly to his head and squeezed a fly that had settled there. Then he dropped it to the sand, and stood on it.

In fact Hector went next to the Egyptian Gendarmerie, and served under Valentine Baker, a reputed friend of the Prince of Wales, who had served a year's sentence in prison for indecently assaulting a young girl in a railway carriage in a Liphook to Waterloo train on a hot June afternoon. He had been a forty-year-old colonel at the time: his victim was a Miss Dickinson aged twenty-two, of respectable background, who had accused him of indecent advances. As a result of this episode he was cashiered from the army but later became a Turkish mercenary before taking command of the Gendarmerie. (Kitchener was to fall in love with his daughter, Hermione, perhaps the only female love of his life. She was aged sixteen at the time, and Kitchener was thirty-three, but there was no formal engagement. She died aged eighteen of typhoid fever in Cairo. At times Kitchener wore under his shirt a locket given to him by Valentine Baker, which contained a miniature portrait of Hermione.)

In spite of Baker's peculiar reputation Hector got on well with him, but in any case he was not to be with him permanently. While with him, however, he began to mould fellahin troops into a fighting force and was then transferred to the Egyptian army with the rank of captain. He also learned Arabic to add to his Gaelic and Urdu. At the battle of Tel el Kebir, Baker was killed and the Gendarmerie disbanded.

Until 1884 there had been only eight battalions of fellahín infantry, but in that year in Suakin on the Red Sea a ninth battalion was formed. Hector was put in charge of it with five British officers under him. So it was that it was these jet-black Sudanese that he trained and drilled in weaponry as they lived in the desert in tents in the most intolerable heat and fire of the day and the chill of the night.

So it was that Hector was promoted, and had very little to spend his money on, and was in action, and all this suited him.

The Sudanese soldiers were very black, very tall, very thin in the arms and legs, but brave, loyal and impulsive. They were fond of music and Hector taught them how to love the bagpipes, and they could play 'Auld Lang Syne' and 'God Save the Queen'. Before battle three freshly killed goats had to be placed on the sand in front of them, the blood drying in the sand while each soldier stepped over them for good fortune.

Hector walked and rode and taught weaponry to the 'blue' men, as they were called. He was indomitable, resolute, patient. He was in his element, even in the intense, brutal heat of the Sudan. He seemed to wear armour under his clothes.

Hector's ethic was that there was no man who could not be taught. His spindly-legged battalion was to be made to approach that Platonic ideal he had in his mind. Sometimes they rebelled, often they hated him, but they grew to respect and love him.

He surprised his officers, for he would take over the drilling himself. He called the black men by Gaelic names. Sometimes he would shout 'Angus', and a tall, spindly-legged fellow would approach.

'Angus,' he would say, 'you're not so good today, are you? You'll have to do better than that, Angus.' And he would stroke his face gently, looking into his eyes. Then his voice would rise to a shout and he would shout, 'Angus, YOU'LL HAVE TO DO BETTER THAN THAT!' (This in Arabic, which the officers didn't understand.)

His voice would roar across the parade ground, 'Iain, you're not being correct, are you?' And a black man would turn and listen.

'It's the only way,' he would say to his officers. 'Drill, drill, drill. No end of drill, till they've got it coming out of their ears. You can make a soldier out of anyone if you work at it.'

It seemed as if they didn't have NCOs at all, for Hector would do all the drill himself.

'Sergeant,' he would say, 'never give up. Keep going. That is the secret. There is one thing wrong with them yet, they are too impulsive. They must be trained to follow commands.'

The desert itself was sometimes mountainous dunes, sometimes beautifully sculpted. It could be dusty with sandstones, it could stretch for flat featureless miles. It could be rose-coloured, intangible. It had pale green scorpions, snakes. The dunes might look like whales, barren, powdery, lifeless. It could be golden or red. At night it could be so cold that the teeth chattered. In the daytime one would dream of ice-cold water while travelling across it. Shadows in the sand were sometimes blue. It gave an impression of infinite space. It could be enchanting, demonic, blank.

Hector drilled and drilled. Attention, left turn, right turn. He cajoled, threatened. At first his company looked like a lifeless palisade, mechanical, without spirit. What did this man want of them? they thought. All must be correct, uniforms must be correct. Without discipline the world was without form, that was Hector's ethic. But they did not share his dream. At first they did not care who they fought for, the Dervishes or the Egyptian army. They would smile affably, equably; they were like children, often gay for no reason, sometimes gloomy. Their moods changed as the moods of children change.

They preferred the bayonet to the rifle. The bayonet was more physical. Also they were liable to fire indiscriminately. Often Hector despaired of them but he remained resolute, grim, strong. If he reprimanded them they would smile ingratiatingly at him. But he would not let them escape into their shadowy recesses. He would follow them, transform them. They were affectionate, changeable, like the shadows that bloomed in the desert, which were sometimes dull, sometimes saffron-coloured. He would sometimes shout at them in Arabic, sometimes, forgetting himself, in Gaelic. He was eagle-eyed, missing nothing. They felt him as a perpetual invasion of themselves. Even in the heat of the day he was indomitable, inexhaustible. He appeared as an enemy in their fluid dreams. Their immediate spontaneous nature hated him, withdrew from him, wanted him to go away, to leave them alone. But he would not let go.

He knew them individually, for he had been brought up in a world where this was natural. One time he was riding ahead of them and heard some of them plotting to kill him. 'When we have a battle we will kill him,' they were saying among each other. They didn't know that he understood. Suddenly he turned towards them, and said in Arabic, 'Why don't you do it now? You are many, I am one. You have bayonets and rifles. What's stopping you?'

They gazed up at him, astounded. But they were silent. They didn't attempt to kill him, for he seemed like a god.

Later he told his officers about the incident.

'Well, you do drive them,' they said.

'They have to be driven. The point is, they didn't kill me. They ought to have killed me, perhaps. Perhaps that is a failure on my part that they didn't.' And he gazed at them with his Highland wisdom and they gazed uncomprehendingly back. Why did the man never fall ill? they used to think. Some of them did, and he didn't. If he fell ill he would send the doctor away. 'No, I haven't time just now,' he would say. And the illness would fall away from him as if by magic. They admired him, but they weren't interested in drill in the way he was. That was for the NCOs, not for officers. Anyway, working with blacks was a bit demeaning, though Hector didn't feel like that. How could you become noticed at the head of a blue-black army?

The prospective plotters didn't say anything; they were astonished, rooted to the spot. Their shadows slanted in thin lines across the desert. Hector turned away contemptuously. He was never in his life frightened of death. But in his inflexible rage for order, which he felt would confer dignity on them, he hadn't understood their resentment. He had made the mistake of thinking that they wanted what he wanted. Their fluid tribal natures disliked his abstractionism.

Yet he was there, he was unchanging, he was strong: he seemed sufficient to himself. Two cultures: a supple, variable, feminine one met a rational demanding one. It was inevitable that they should succumb to his certainty. Sometimes he would use one

80

of them against the other: 'Look what he can do. Can you not do the same?' His strength was unchanging because he absolutely believed in what he was doing, and not only that, but more deeply in the abstract beauty of what he was doing. Sometimes at night he watched the swarming starry sky, blazingly illuminated, each star in its proper place, an inevitable orderly procession, and it gave him a mystic sense of order. It was overwhelming, almost holy. He was their moon, they were his many stars. When their rifles clicked as one, that was mystic gratification. When they marched in step with vivacity and not mechanically, that too was mystic harmony.

Sometimes he would think of his father who would say to him, as they worked on a house together, 'You put that stone there, don't you see?'

In his dream of harmony he forgot about the sun: it was as if it wasn't there at all. He ignored the heat and dust, the large pitiless flies. Each morning was a revelation to him; he was untiring. He would create an army out of this barren desert which was hostile, inhuman.

At first their shooting was not good, the rifles wavered, as their arms were not strong. But the rifle was not immediate enough for them anyway. To keep them in square, that would be difficult. It wasn't that they were frightened, not at all; rather, they would make a passionate disorderly assault on the enemy. Cold calculation, waiting, was not in their nature. Like cats they wanted to leap at the enemy, to feel his flesh. The rifle was abstract and set a distance between them and their foe. It was hard for them not to make their rushes.

At times their open defenceless gaiety enchanted him, but he hardened his heart. There would be sudden outbursts of laughter from their tents. They would sing some of their songs. They would chatter endlessly. He felt that a gulf lay between them and him. Sometimes they would ask him if he was displeased with them. He sensed too that they sometimes laughed at him. Was it not better to sit and tell stories of formal antique quality? What did this relentless ferocity of his mean? Time was what they lived in, it was not what they used. Sometimes they thought their commander was unhappy. Why else was he so busy? What a restless, endlessly

81

busy life he led. They themselves were not ambitious, not at all gnawed by pictures of themselves in higher positions. Ambition was a long-term idea which didn't manifest itself to them.

What they did was to try to please him, since he had more will than they had, and because they honoured him. They recognised courage when they saw it. He was their father, their supremely strong father. Their inexhaustible father. If he wanted them to do incomprehensible things, they would do them with willingness. They would try not to rush forward, though that was hard. They would try to learn something of his eternal composure, though that was hard too.

And like a god he grew to be pleased with them. And the more they grew like him, the more they loved him. They changed, though they did not know it. They no longer wished to kill him, though his relentlessness was as great as ever. They sensed the idea in him as a concrete thing. The idea was part of him, without it he was nothing. They stepped across an invisible borderline, and he was waiting open-armed for them on the other side, glad that at last they had arrived. They grew readier than they were, they were no longer like a painted palisade. They loved marching to the pipes, there was good humour and fellowship in their ranks. They delighted in the security that his order had given them. They felt safe with his demands; they had lost a great deal but they stretched out for the next thing. They were almost ready.

They fought the Dervishes at Gemaizeh, and routed them, along with another battalion. They weren't frightened of the Dervishes at all. And the Dervish commander suddenly realised that he wasn't facing the old Egyptian army which broke easily, but a hard, tough instrument. They did – because they were not quite ready – make an unauthorised rush, and at one point Hector had to shout at them in Gaelic, 'Thigibh air ais a sin, a chlann na bids! (Come back from there, you sons of bitches)', but they hadn't been beaten. They wanted to throw themselves on the Dervishes to feel their mortal flesh. He was so angry and so disheartened at one point that they came to him and stroked his knees and said, 'Do not be frightened, do not be frightened,' and he burst out laughing. But in general, apart from the unauthorised rush, they were disciplined and ferocious and drove the Dervishes back.

82

And Hector himself was at home in the fire of war again. And proud of the instrument he had fashioned, those spindly-legged, jet-black soldiers, who looked so much like something out of a negro music-hall troupe.

And Hector was promoted to major and given medals of all kinds, including the DSO.

After the battle his officers were astonished to see him take his men out on to the parade ground to give them an extra drill.

'This is unbelievable,' said one of them to the other.

And the other said, 'Well, it's his way, old boy. Everything goes together.' But they had noticed how angry he had been at the casualties, as if he should never have lost anyone, as if he had trained them well enough for them not to have allowed themselves to be killed, as if the death of one was a failure of his ideal.

So they came on him sitting in his tent, his eyes wet, though he was immediately his affable self again.

'Poor Angus's gone,' he said to them as they were leaving. None of them knew who Angus was, for they all looked the same to them.

'They must all be buried,' Hector would shout, as he looked at the illimitable sand. 'They must all be buried.' And they heard him muttering under his breath, 'These bloody Dervishes.'

Sometimes, if he was in a relaxed mood, Hector would talk to his officers about other than military matters. He would mention, for instance, how Arabs lived in tribes as Highlanders in clans, how the Highlanders too would fight each other with great cruelty. He saw the Empire as a unifying power which would enforce peace.

In connection with this he would say that although he had been brought up to speak Gaelic, he would prefer to see one language – English – spoken throughout the Empire. Languages were divisive. The Empire would be unified by one language. There was a time when Bonnie Prince Charles had tried to conquer Britain, but that had been an adventurous aberration. It was lucky that he hadn't won. There was no harm in going to different parts of the world. He himself had a brother in Devon and another in London and another in Australia.

'I never liked crofting,' he would say. 'Our lives were harsh and the land was poor. We lived in small houses with thatched roofs. I always wanted to get away from home into the wide world. I dreamed of that when I was young. Our school was small too and we had to bring peat for the fire. I used to fight a lot and play tricks on people. At the end of the school day we often used to divide ourselves into teams and throw stones at each other.

'I read a lot. I have been a great student. And I advise you to do the same. I've learned Urdu and some Arabic. I used to study the army regulations even before I joined the army.

'I worked in a shop that sold tweeds. I found that very boring, though the shopkeeper was good to me. I've always regretted that I ran away from his shop without telling him. But that was in the days of my youth when I didn't think of others.

'If I hadn't joined the army, what would I have been now? I might have been a crofter living very frugally and seeing no return for my daily toil. The Highlands of Scotland have always been poor. It would be better if more left so that the ones who remain could live better.'

The officers liked and respected him. But for the most part they did not know what he was talking about. They knew nothing about crofts, they could not imagine the circumstances in which he had grown up. They found him a decisive perfectionist, but humane. He had an easy manner which he had learned in the classless society where he grew up and which allowed him to make instant contact with his black soldiers. They couldn't understand his fanatic interest in drill, but he seemed to understand the Sudanese soldiers better than they did.

'Discipline,' he would say, 'is everything. Absolutely everything. If you don't have discipline in an army you have nothing.

'Discipline must be strong so that an army can stand its ground unflinchingly till the command for firing is given. The Highlanders were defeated at Culloden because they made undisciplined rushes against a modern disciplined army. The opposing general simply made his army wait and let them fire at the last moment. Steadiness arises from discipline and is vital. If I had been a general I would have taught the Highland army discipline first and last. Our soldiers here are like the Highlanders. They would like to throw their rifles away and charge with the bayonet. We will have to make sure that they don't do that.'

Words seemed to come from his mouth like solid stones. His mind was not quick but it was strong and it fixed on a few motifs and themes. They had seen he had no fear and they admired him for that.

'I want to tell you something,' he would say. 'The non-commissioned officers are the backbone of the army. They are responsible for discipline and discipline is simply repetition. You must train a soldier as if you were training a dog to round up sheep. Soldiers must respond to commands instantly.'

They listened to him but they were not wholly convinced. They were not on the whole interested in the work that discipline demanded. Sergeants belonged to a different world from their own. They felt that what the sergeants were doing was not pukka: training black soldiers was inferior work. Why, all they were doing was whipping savages into shape. They did not think of them as human beings at all.

Many of them didn't like the desert. They didn't find it romantic: for a great deal of the time it was a hot hell-house. There were fevers, there were large horrible flies. Hector didn't suffer from fevers; his vision and work sustained him.

They couldn't understand how the tribes of the desert lived, but Hector could. He could imagine them gathering round a fire at night and telling each other stories, much as had been done in the Highlands. Then they had a rigid concept of honour, as the Highlanders had. He told them about the Massacre of Glencoe: how the worst part of that was that the Campbells had accepted the hospitality of the Macdonalds before slaughtering them. The idea of hospitality had been outraged. The Arabs too had a clear concept of hospitality. They were sudden and quick to anger. They would have their hereditary beliefs, their hereditary customs. They would be as brave as the Highlanders were.

He had no longing for his home. To him the stars were brilliant companies inhabiting the sky. His sense of duty was strong. He had been given a task and he must do it. His will must keep the battalion unified. Sometimes he thought of his wife in a distant way. In the desert, however, it seemed that Scotland, Britain, was a dream, that his marriage was a dream.

Sometimes he would stare across the desert which he would populate with his dreams. It changed its lights continually as the Highlands did. He thought of Cairo, of the pyramids, of the Nile with its feluccas, of the peasants eternally bowed under burdens. He recalled the little glancing boats, the egrets. He hadn't particularly liked the winding, stinking streets of Cairo, the Egyptians' treatment of their animals, the sly, furtive townspeople. He liked this desert silence, its nocturnal illuminated holy hush.

Oh, at times it would take all his will-power to combat the heat, the flies, the dust, the sand. The battalion depended on his will-power to keep it in motion; it wasn't easy, but he mustn't show tiredness, indecision to his men.

His vision was of an Empire which would encompass the world. Its laws and its language would be equal. Its red colour would embrace the earth and he would be happy to be its servant. At the moment he was like someone in the Bible in his tent, reading a book, a shepherd of these people, a kind of Abraham. That was his task for the moment and he would execute it to the best of his ability.

And so he fought at Gemaizeh and at Toski. He became a notable figure, calm and solid, among these skirmishes and battles. While the Dervishes, white-robed and fanatical, poured extravagantly against the British square in an immense din and confusion, he was like a statue on his horse, steady and composed.

Hector felt pride in this instrument he had created by will-power and undeviating determination in this indolent land. In the dust and heat it remained steadfast. It returned to him the love that he lavished on it. It was respected, feared. In the smell of burning leather and smoke it remained immovable. As for Hector himself war was his natural setting. He was happy to be away from the hierarchies of the Mess, and its artificial rules. He was happy that he did not have to worry about money. It never occurred to him that he might be killed. Cutting his way through Dervishes, he felt invincible. Sometimes he even pitied the enemy. How, without discipline, could they prevail? How could their raging, swirling bodies survive the white heat of discipline and order? Like vicious ghosts they charged out of the dust and like ghosts they lay on the sand. (Though at times they could be patient and cunning too, and they had good leaders.)

Sometimes at night he would imagine their bodies like glittering sheaves in the moonlight, torn by jackals. They reminded him of the sheaves of corn at home lying in the moonlight, a peaceful harvest. Disorder, however, had to be quelled by order. Disorder was failure of the ideal. The ideal was an ordered silence such as the desert revealed under its brilliant nocturnal lights. He would think, There was some error that my men made today. I must correct it. The error was like a sin that disturbed him. In it perhaps his Presbyterian ancestry spoke. And the desert honed down to a minimum was his natural setting. He was often tired, even *his* body was not inexhaustible, but of course he never complained.

An enormous surge of love flowed out from him to his Sudanese soldiers. He could not be said to have loved his wife in the same way. This love arose from a common danger shared; it was a creative, continually present love. Sometimes he would touch them and his hand would recoil as if from electricity. They were his children, his mysterious children, torn out of a mysterious past. The sheen of their bodies too was mysterious and strange as if the night had become close and beautiful.

When they died, part of him died. Surely men could be made invulnerable by discipline, he often thought. At the very limits of discipline there was safety, indestructibility. He was angry with them for having got killed. Their deaths were a fundamental disobedience.

If, in the heat of battle, he saw a Dervish gutting one of his men with a knife, his rage became boundless. These are my men, you mustn't touch them. After a battle he became moody and morose. It had been proved to him yet again that discipline was fallible.

Though his lips were often swollen and dry with thirst, he wouldn't complain. Though his body sometimes shook with fever, he didn't complain. It seemed as if he was indestructible. The desert too must be conquered. Beautiful in its changing colours, ugly in its stones and manifestation of stinging insects, a hell-hole of heat, it too must be conquered. And the Dervishes must be swept from it, as his mother used to sweep the floor clean, till it had a poor but pristine quality.

He hated the Dervishes as they hacked away at horses' legs, at camels' legs, as their hating eyes glared up at him, as if he were an interruption to their heaven where they would feast for ever more. He hated them for their viciousness, for infringing the limits of order. They were like the insects, irritable, always present. They affronted him. Against their fanatical religious dogma he set the fanatical dogma of his discipline. The instrument of Empire, himself deeply deceived, he strode this livid theatre of action uncomplainingly.

Let the other officers of the line despise him for leading nig-nogs, savages: he knew he had created the instrument that he himself led. Which of them could say that? No white ghosts would be allowed to annihilate his black spindly-legged men. They might worship other gods, but there was nothing he could do about that. In their secretive blackness, they might giggle and tell each other secrets, but that did not bother him.

He did not mind if he died in this desert with its ferocious stitching of insects and its ancient tranquillity. Not that he wished to die, but this place might be as good as any. Sometimes he talked of death with his officers. They wanted to die, if at all, in glory and dazzle. But they felt inferior to officers of the line in a way that he did not.

He himself did not care how he died. 'The time will come, it is inevitable,' he would say, shrugging his shoulders. He was in fact echoing the voice of his mother who would often say, 'We never know the day or the hour.' Like so many of her people she bowed to death as to a creel on her shoulders. Some of course talked of Gordon and how he had died like a prepared bride. But in those years as they passed he didn't feel mortal, for his work was not finished.

The desert enchanted him. It was as if it was inhabited by sacred prophets from the Old Testament. It was a treasury of strangeness. Sometimes among the sand and stones, you would suddenly see flowers spring up after showers. Miracles of resurrection. If death was as fruitful as the desert sometimes was, it could be easily borne. For the desert was not death, though sometimes it might appear so. It pulsed with life, with snakes, lizards, jackals, foxes. Birds of prey slanted over it.

The desert suited him; he donned it like a uniform and it returned to him its passionate, austere love.

And the years passed in endless skirmishes and marches.

10

ECTOR watched his men toiling away at the railway, carrying big planks between them in the hot sun. These menial tasks were not what they were used to, but they were cheerful enough.

A stocky man with a moustache and wearing a white hat came over to him. 'Busy scene,' he said. 'Kitchener obviously means business. Oh, by the way, my name's Griffiths. I'm a correspondent. You're Mac, aren't you? I've heard of you. These yours?' he said, pointing at the toiling Sudanese.

'Yes.'

'Don't suppose you could give me an interview?'

'I don't think so,' said Hector.

'Didn't think you would. Kitchener's not fond of correspondents. I don't know why.'

Hector said nothing.

'In fact,' said Griffiths, 'I saw him not so long ago shouting at some of the workers. He's very impatient.'

And, looking out at the gunboats, 'The engine of one of his new toys blew up and he nearly blew his gasket. He's very aloof, isn't he? Mind you, I did some research on him. He's Irish, of course, and named after Horatio Nelson. In Cairo they don't like him much. No time for small talk.

'They're really black, aren't they?' he continued, glancing at the toiling Sudanese. 'Really, really black.'

'They're good soldiers,' said Hector.

'They could do with better boots,' said Griffiths. 'Kitchener cuts everything to the bone, doesn't he? In fact there he is, surrounded by his young officers. The rising Hamlet.' And he

90

sniffed contemptuously. 'Naturally he would know about railways. He's an engineer. Did you know that his father was an eccentric colonel who made his sons sleep on newspapers instead of sheets? It's amazing what one can find out when one sets out to do it. Maybe that's why he dislikes us poor correspondents.' And he laughed. 'You were pointed out to me. You've been here for a long while, haven't you?'

'Quite a while,' said Hector. 'But I don't want you to write anything about me particularly.'

'Mustn't draw attention away from the star, eh?' said Griffiths, taking out a cigar and sticking it in his mouth. 'Can appreciate that. Still, I suppose there'll be plenty to write about shortly when the war really gets going. The idea of a railway is brilliant, I must admit. Pity he isn't liked more by the common soldier. I talked to a few of them and they said they could do with better clothes and equipment. Everything's run on the cheap.'

Suddenly one of the Sudanese ran over to Hector and said, 'We've found water, bey.'

'Good,' said Hector. 'That's very good.' And the Sudanese soldier ran back again.

'They seem very fond of you,' said Griffiths.

'Oh, I don't know about that,' said Hector guardedly. He really didn't want to put himself forward in any way. For one thing he knew that Kitchener was an egotist who didn't like attention drawn away from himself. He didn't like the way in which the correspondent was watching himself and the blacks. He might make a long romantic story about his sojourn in the desert. One had to be careful with these people.

'Kitchener's a good, determined soldier. He will avenge Gordon. Maybe you should talk to him.'

'He won't speak to me,' said Griffiths with a sigh, flicking his ash on to the sand where his hat was perfectly delineated. 'But he's certainly an organiser, they say. Everyone's agreed on that. On the other hand, I'm not convinced that he's a Horatio Nelson. He won't take any risks. On the other hand, perhaps that's what's needed. What are these Dervishes like? You've fought them, haven't you?'

'They're not cowards,' said Hector diplomatically.

'I've heard that they don't care if they die or not. They believe in some sort of heaven of their own.'

Hector shifted in the hot sun. Sweat was pouring down the back of his neck. He wished he could dress as lightly as this correspondent. The sky was a clear blue above him. In front of him the blacks toiled, staggering under the weight of the planks with their spidery legs.

And behind it all one could sense Kitchener's driving will.

'I find it quite easy to talk to you,' said Griffiths, smiling, 'even though you are telling me nothing, and I respect you for that. I'm of Welsh extraction myself and you're Scottish. Don't be afraid, I won't write you up. I know there are correspondents who lie and cheat, but I'm not one of them. I'm not really, you know.' And he turned his calm blue eyes on Hector. For a moment they seemed to match the blue of the sky. 'I've heard people say that you've worked your way up from a private. That's right, isn't it?'

'Yes,' said Hector briefly.

'That must have been interesting.' He waited, but Hector didn't add anything to what he had said.

'I mean, a lot of these officers don't care much for their men, and Kitchener apparently is a prime example. But you obviously do.'

Still Hector said nothing.

Suddenly Griffiths' face broke into a brilliant smile and he said, 'I take that back about finding it easy to talk to you. Nevertheless we Celts sense much without being told. Best of luck anyway,' and he tipped his hat as he went away. Hector watched him for a while and then went to help some of his men who were finding trouble with a plank. Naturally he had to be careful what he said. He didn't want any of Kitchener's glory to be deflected away from him. He had heard it said that Kitchener was a ruthless man who made surprise visits to officers in key stations. And also that he suffered from painful headaches and didn't sleep much. Hector had never had a headache in his life. In some ways he had never felt better.

Except for – well – except for Christine and his son who were so far away and so unreal. So terribly unreal . . . He hadn't seen them for years; 1892 it was, when he had his last leave. He had played clumsily with his five-year-old Hector who had pulled daringly at his ill-fitting civilian jacket, and who had appeared to him less real than his Sudanese soldiers. After a while the domestic world irritated him, it certainly lacked the splendour of the desert. He felt enclosed and in some deep way diminished, as if part of his real self were being drained away.

It seemed to him as if both he and Christine had changed, as if . . . well, as if – a terrible thought occurred to him – as if these black soldiers were his children now. I don't wish to go back to Britain, he thought. If Griffiths knew of my secret marriage he would have a good story. Behind this stolid exterior, he might write, there is, well, what is there? An unfaithful husband? No, not that. Merely a sense of unreality except where the army is concerned, where guns and swords are concerned.

He sighed and looked towards Kitchener who was standing surrounded by his adoring young officers. It was known that even Kitchener had once been in love, but his loved one had died. Why, like himself, he thought, he couldn't imagine Kitchener being in love with a real live woman. He could no longer see Griffiths. He hoped that he hadn't managed to get a story out of his few meagre words, though some of these correspondents could be very ruthless and deceptive.

While the railway was snaking its way across the desert, Hector and General Hunter – a man superior in rank to Hector, though younger than him – were continually marching and fighting. Sometimes they marched through the darkness of sandstorms when hardly anything was visible, and sand filled their mouths and infiltrated their clothes, and all the world seemed to be a moving grave of sand. There was hardly any light; there was nothing but sand.

At other times they were almost paralysed by illnesses – shiverings, diarrhoea – so that marching was almost impossible. These illnesses might have been caused by the water they drank and which they had to drink because of the heat. Rotting camels' bodies lay in pools but they still bent down, seeing their meagre faces reflected, and drank, shivering. Camels' heads seemed to mock them: 'This is what you will come to,' they said.

In the heat too they were troubled by mirages. Trees suddenly grew ahead of them, towering and green. Water, clear and abundant, shone in front of them. And the spindly-legged men staggered towards it.

Mirages, sickness, sandstorms, thirst made their lives miserable. It was at times a country of the damned, prolific of fresh tortures. Their food was full of sand grains and so were their shoes. The sky would suddenly darken as if they were in hell. And their mouths swelled with thirst.

On the better days they swept into places like Firket and Dongola and the scattered village of Berber, and drove the inhabitants away. They came out of the desert like avengers, among the poor mud huts with their palm-leaf roofs, and a lot of the time found the villages empty as if the villagers had been warned of their coming. They destroyed the houses and set fire to the roofs. Out of the sandstorms, out of the mirages they came with swords and guns, thin-faced conquerors, with fire and steel.

Sometimes in the extraordinary mirages Hector would see his wife standing. She was saying to him, 'All you think about is your army and your soldiers,' and he knew it was true. They had nothing to say to each other; he wished to be away among his silent tents. There was no love between them. There was something untidy about that civilian shoddiness. He was no longer lonely, he had his soldiers to return to, and she was jealous of them. He hated that feminine world, there were too many recriminations, shoutings. He wasn't in control of his life there.

Thus from the mirages, from the starry sky, she stood out at him, blaming him. And he struck out at the enemy, their villages, their huts; he drove them further into the desert. Let them survive there if they could. Others were sick; he wasn't. Masked in the sandstorm he was still strong. Once he saw a child running away from a hut looking over its shoulder, and he stood there for a moment, astonished.

He and Hunter got on well. They would talk about Kitchener, saying that eventually Gordon's bare skull would be avenged.

'Gordon once fought against a Chinese religious fanatic like the Mahdi,' Hunter told him. 'And they brought him the skull of a prisoner after he had specifically ordered mercy. He was very angry.'

And now it was Gordon's skull that inhabited Kitchener's mind and his days and nights of espionage. Victory with their gunboats and railway was almost inevitable, though the camels' heads stared out of poisonous pools, though the sand was a continual irritation, though the green trees leaned deceptively towards them, though the sun blazed down on them and sweat poured from their bodies. The varieties of the desert's discomforts were a continual astonishment to them.

Kitchener and Mahmud faced each other at Atbara, the river behind Mahmud alive with crocodiles. Mahmud's army was hidden by thorns and reinforced by a zariba barricade. Kitchener approached at night and determined to attack at dawn, though he had a superstitious dread of Fridays. Unknown to Mahmud he had reinforced his army with Warwicks, Lincolns, Camerons and Seaforths. At about six in the morning the shells from the ships began to hit the zariba, and Kitchener made his usual frontal attack. Each soldier in Kitchener's army had a Lee Matford Mark II, and the artillery had been reinforced by the Maxim gun, and there were also canister shells containing bullets which burst on impact. There was a battery of Howitzers capable of firing lyddite – high explosive shells. Then there were dum-dum bullets which tore through the body on impact.

The Dervishes, incarcerated in thorns, had ageing Martini-Henry breech loaders, antique elephant guns, swords, daggers, lances. The bombardment was tremendous, helped by rocket projectiles from the ships on the river.

Hector's Sudanese were in the centre of the advancing formation, side by side with the Camerons, as volleys from the Dervishes hit them while Hunter and Hector rode ahead.

Eventually it was hand-to-hand fighting in the trenches on that murderous morning. Many blacks were found chained by both legs and hands to the trenches, guns in their hands, their faces turned to the enemy, some with forked sticks at their backs. As usual the Sudanese fought well against the Dervishes who were sustained by their fanatical religion. Kitchener's head cleared of its thorny migraines. The battle continued. The Sudanese had been the first in the trenches: they fought furiously among the pits and ditches.

Hector felt an enormous pride. His troops were proving themselves to be at least as good as the other troops, fighting passionately with the bayonet against a fierce enemy. The red sun was rising on the red carnage among the thorns. The bayonets stabbed among antique swords, blood flowed among the pits and trenches. A vicious face suddenly appeared, and he stabbed.

Then it was all over. The crocodiles fed well as bodies drifted into the river. There was a silence into which the Highland troops chased Mahmud's troops across the cobbles. The guns had stopped, and Hector saw around him bodies caught in the last ferocious rictus of death. As if in slow motion he saw the Highland troops gaining on the Dervishes, arms falling and rising.

Mahmud remained alive. Kitchener, as ruthless as the enemy, determined to make an example of the leader, partly in order to show the native troops that he was after all mortal. He made a triumphant march through Berber, with General Hunter beside him. He rode a white horse, accompanied by the native brigade. Behind him was Mahmud, his hands behind his back, his feet fettered, proud, tall, fearless – he was about forty years of age. There was Highland music on the bagpipes, and music hall tunes from the brass band.

Hector, who was five years older than his prisoner, watched as Mahmud was made sometimes to run, sometimes to walk, while laughing Sudanese soldiers made fun of him. Their teeth were white and shining in the sun.

He didn't feel any pity for Mahmud. Mahmud was the enemy of the British Empire. Mahmud was publicly humiliated as a psychological gesture to show the superiority of Kitchener's army.

Mahmud remained proud and silent. Kitchener radiated sunniness and success. He would be the new darling of Britain who had risen like a star shell out of the battle. He was a new, meticulous, almost Teutonic force. But worse had happened to Gordon than to Mahmud who was chained like a slave and made to dance in his fetters. The successful Kitchener and his officers rode tall above him under an empty sky. Allah had failed Mahmud, as was intended. New technology had attacked the will of Allah or perhaps Allah had been angry with his servants.

Kitchener stared inflexibly ahead. Like a stricken, misshapen shadow, Mahmud shuffled lamely behind him. Kitchener suddenly said to Hunter and Hector, 'It would have been worse if we had lost.' Then he was silent again. His white horse gleamed in the sunlight, not a ghost but a signal of the triumph of the white race.

They rode through Berber, a fairly large though mean town, with, however, good land between the houses and the river. It stretched for about seven miles. There was a rank smell from it.

Bright birds flew around the river; the sated crocodiles slept. Through the stinking village the horses cantered. The Sudanese laughed and giggled as they mocked the fettered prisoner.

After Atbara the army rested, waiting for the Nile to rise to allow the ships to get over the cataracts. White birds flew above the river; crocodiles drowsed, their great jaws inert.

On 24 August the army moved up the west bank of the Nile, 8,200 British and 17,000 Egyptian and Sudanese troops. Hector commanded a brigade. Kitchener had forty-four pieces of field artillery and twenty Maxims. On the ships of the Nile he had thirty-six guns and twenty-four Maxims.

Gunboats began to bombard Omdurman; great holes were made in the Mahdi's white tomb. There was a marvellous brutal contempt about the onslaught, as if from a distance there was no immunity for the Dervishes. Breaches appeared in the city walls, punched by an invisible enemy.

While this was happening, Hector stood beside his ADC, Lieutenant Pritchard, who said, 'It'll still be tough, sir.'

'Yes,' said Hector absently.

He saw Kitchener standing by himself, field-glasses trained on Omdurman, and at the same time heard the gunners loudly competing as to which of their guns had hit the tomb. The temperature was well over 100 degrees.

Then Hector nodded, 'This will be it.'

Later, he with others watched in amazement as the Dervish army flooded out on to the plain in front with Omdurman. What had caused them to do that? But in truth there seemed to be countless numbers of them.

That night Hector couldn't sleep. Would the Dervish army attack in darkness? Their own army was drawn up in a semi-circle with its back to the river. Would the enemy army try to sweep them into the river at night?

Also the enemy drums beat all night, the copper war drums, as well as the mournful sound of the obeya, the horn made from the tusk of an elephant. Searchlights roamed the field, and he wondered what the Dervishes made of them. Did they think of them as predatory rays hunting for them?

He wondered who else was lying awake in that tormenting noise. Kitchener, certainly. There was little point in sleeping, anyway. He thought of a dreadful scenario of camels and mules panicking in a confused battle, and the Dervishes driving them to the river.

At 3.30 a.m. the army stirred and stood to arms. At 6.40 a.m. the shouting of the Dervishes became audible. At 6.45 a.m. Kitchener's field artillery opened fire on 10,000 Dervishes who with white banners attacked the left and centre. They poured towards the British army and as they poured they fell; they were mown down, scythed, and lay in sheaves of ghostly white in the dawn. They breasted an enormous wave of fire which shook them, lifted them from the ground. Hector thought, this is like Culloden. So too did the Highlanders pour towards Cumberland's fatal guns. The battle was a massacre. The Dervishes withdrew shortly after 8 a.m., leaving 2,000 dead.

Kitchener advanced towards Khartoum, Hector's brigade slightly to the rear. What Kitchener in his confident advance didn't know was that there were Dervishes concealed to his rear. First, there came an army with black banners against Hector. He fought them off with concentrated gunfire, trying to calm his excited men.

Then, after these had been desperately fought off, there appeared an army with green banners. If the black and green armies had arrived simultaneously, as had been the plan, Hector would have had no chance at all. As it was, he had a short time to arrange fresh dispositions.

Absolutely calm, with the rigour of the trained sergeant, he wrote his hieroglyphics, his plan of battle, in the sand with his stick. At that very point, in that very moment, his training, his discipline, his experiences as an NCO flowered miraculously into existence. Under fire, he swung his brigade to meet the new threat. It was as if he was on a parade ground, it was as if there was no enemy there, as he worked out his tactics. He had to move his battalions one after the other from a line facing the west to one facing the north, towards the streaming green banners. He was cool, composed, certain. This was exactly the moment he had been created for. This was what his study of the army manuals in his shop in Inverness had taught him. The fire of the Sudanese, which had been almost random, became concentrated as Hector rode among them, knocking down their rifles with his stick. They delighted him in that moment. They were his children who were obeying him. His concentration was ferocious. It was as if he had invented a new dance. Gaps began to open among the green banners. The brigade remained steady; Hector rode among them, solid as a rock. He could have shouted with joy as he saw the instrument he had created fire with such coolness.

Then the green banners began to retreat, defeated by the steady fire and also by the coming Lincolns. By 11.25 a.m. the Dervish attack had been repulsed.

Later, correspondents were to write about that amazing fight of Hector's and to say that Kitchener had been saved (the odious Kitchener who was always rude to them, even to the young Churchill).

One of them wrote:

But the cockpit of the fight was Macdonald's . . . To meet [the attack] he turned his front through a complete half-circle facing successively south, west and north. Every tactician in the army was delirious in his praise; the ignorant correspondent was content to watch the man and his blacks. 'Cool as on parade' is an old phrase. Beneath the strong square-hewn face you could tell that the brain was working as if packed in ice. He sat stolid on his horse and bent his black brows towards the green flag and the Remingtons. Then he turned to a galloper with an order, and cantered easily up to a battalion commander. Magically the rifles hushed, the stinging powder smoke wisped away, and the companies were rapidly threading back and forward, round and round, in and out, as if it were a figure in a dance. In two minutes the brigade was together in a new place. The field in front was hastening towards us in a whitey-brown cloud of Dervishes. An order! Macdonald's jaws gripped and hardened as the flame spirited out again and the whitey-brown cloud quivered and stood still. He saw everything: knew what to do: how to do it: did it.

A star had arisen, though Hector did not as yet know it and did not see it as he hastened towards Khartoum, watching for a moment the Seaforths plunging into the stream known as Khor Shambar, hitching up their kilts like ballet dancers as they entered the water slow and dirty with the corpses of camels.

Nor did he know it as he watched tears streaming down Kitchener's face at the service held in Gordon's memory outside the ruined palace of Khartoum.

Nor did he know it as Kitchener threw the Mahdi's bones into the Nile only to be forced to retrieve them, and bury the skull secretly at night in a Moslem cemetery.

Though he did know it when Kitchener was given a parliamentary grant of £30,000 and the title of Lord Kitchener of Khartoum, while Hector became a colonel in the British army and a major-general in the Egyptian army, was voted the thanks of the Imperial Parliament, and was made an ADC to the Queen – but was given no money.

After the campaign he wrote to his brother William at Rootfield, his home farm, that he was exhausted from overwork. He had served sixteen years (from 1883 to 1899) in the hell-hole of the Sudan.

He had however become a hero to the Highlanders and among Highland communities in the cities.

For a moment the Empire had trembled and he had saved it. But he did not want to make much of it, for Kitchener was a ruthless man, who did not like rivals.

So he returned again to Britain, to applause such as he had never dreamed of, but with no money, as before. He had saved an Empire (for the Dervishes might have destroyed Kitchener's army from the rear), but while he got many honours, he was very tired after all that service under that relentless sun.

He was proud that his beautiful spontaneous dance had been adopted by the Staff College, but in a way he did not relish meeting the avalanches of praise that awaited him. He was not an orator. And he was sad to leave his Sudanese whom he had made, and who had done what he had asked of them. The last time he met them there were tears streaming down his face. My beloved ones, he thought, you have fought and died for me. What more can a man ask? Their eyes were honest as he embraced them. I love you, he thought, you are my sons, more to me than the son that I have. Maybe I should stay with you, but that is not possible. And in any case how much more of this heat, of these flies, can I bear? And now out of the quietness of the desert I return to the world again. He was like a hermit leaving his cell. At times he dreaded what awaited him. He was not a natural hero like Kitchener or Gordon. He did not have the gift of speech. He did not want to be a hero to the Highlanders starving for someone they could adore after their many losses. There is a desert in my soul, he thought, and it wants to remain inviolate. I wish to remain with my stick-legged black men, with my beloved soldiers, for I am tired, tired . . .

The events that followed were like a dream. The Highlanders gathered him to themselves, overwhelmed him. First there was the Cecil Hotel in London; he heard as if in a dream the names – The Earl of Dunmore, Lord Strathcona, Lord Kingsburgh, Sir James MacGregor, etc., etc., for by that time he could remember no more. The Earl of Atholl presided. There they were in their brilliant kilts, those Highlanders who were making their living in London: and they had chosen him as their hero. The Cockney waiters, plain and meagre in comparison, watched in amazement as these strangely garbed visions planted one foot on the table as they drank a health to Hector.

A man whose name Hector didn't catch, but who was apparently an MP for an English constituency, spoke eloquently and to much applause, saying that it was a 'gran' nicht' for Scotland, the best since Bannockburn. Parliament, he went on, was only a show run by Englishmen, England was really run by Scotland. His beard and flowing hair seemed to grow longer and longer as he spoke, so that he seemed to be a strange vatic prophet conjured out of Highland mists in the middle of London.

The greatest night since Bannockburn, thought Hector, here I was fighting the English after all, though I did not know it.

What a night it was; the haggis, the holy host, was eaten, and the wine was drunk. He was an eagle in the midst of these rainbow-coloured pheasants. The satisfactory ambivalence of it: Let us live in England but pretend that we have fought another Bannockburn. That in fact we are fighting England while staying here. Let us wear our gorgeous raiment of marvellous colours, like Joseph, but we are really running Egypt just the same.

There were more and more speeches, but none that caught the imagination more than the one by the MP.

What do they see in me? thought Hector, the 'man of rock among the gunfire' or whatever. An imperturbable soldier. The 'natural aristocrat', and he smiled grimly. How could he bear this weight, would he not be better back in the desert? What torrential speech did they want him to make? Did they want him to summon them to a revolution?

My own people, he thought, but the Sudanese were my own people too. The rock swayed in the midst of that devoted storm.

No, he must make a simple speech. That was what they expected. Modestly he praised the artillery which was so useful to the modern army. He was saying, 'I am not a hero. I am a soldier and soldiering is my craft.' But the simpler he was, the more attuned he was to what they required of him. After all, statues didn't speak at all. *I do not wish to feel this stone cloak on my shoulders. And already I feel it and it is not comfortable.*

102

And my simple words create a silence around me. I am the strong, silent man. Their faces surrounded him like predatory beings.

(And in the middle of it he thought of Christine and his son. I cannot now, he thought, reveal my secret marriage. Not now. The newspaper reporters would descend on her, and she would hate it. I am now a being, somewhat like Kitchener in England, greater than any ordinary being, and he felt that twist in his stomach again. To find out that he had disobeyed orders and married. What would that do to him now? The higher he climbed the more secretive he must become. To find out that the exemplary soldier had after all cheated! And his in-laws in Edinburgh to be invaded as well. There was no end to the probings of these reporters. I must be grateful to her that she hasn't spoken. But I do not love her, I have withdrawn again into this dream. Everything is a justification for keeping away from her. And she stood in front of him among the smoke, smiling sardonically. I could not stand the loneliness in Edinburgh, and this was the result.)

What a night of wine and speeches. Someone mentioned that he hadn't been given a grant of money from Parliament, that the matter should be pursued. Even they, after all, didn't control Parliament.

And not long afterwards they presented him with a sword of honour themselves. The handle and guard and the bands of the scabbard were solid gold modelled on Celtic lines. On one side of the hilt was the figure of a Highland soldier and on the other that of a Sudanese. In the centre of the guard was the letter M, and on the other the Scottish and the Egyptian flags enamelled in colours. Each point of the guard took the form of a thistle, in the flower of which was a finely cut cairngorm. The scabbard was decorated with appropriate crests, mottoes, arms and orders. The blade was steel of the finest temper with runic ornamentation, spaces being filled in with the Macdonald arms, the crescent and star, the sphinx and an inscription.

Hector gazed at it with amazement. What a beautiful, elegant, perfect instrument – but no money. It would have been vulgar to give money to a 'natural aristocrat'.

And yet he was also a simple peasant son, like Burns himself. He was their bronze idol from the East.

Later a drunken man with wet eyes took him by the hand, and said, 'I have shaken the hand of Hector Macdonald himself,' before staggering away. Oh, the hem of my garment, Hector thought wryly. Someone showed him what the *Northern Weekly* had written about him: 'It is ever so with the true Highlander, bold as an eagle and firm as a rock, and meek as a child.' Never so many similes!

And later, after the hotel had emptied its rainbow-coloured clients on to the streets of London, the dream continued. He would find himself waking up in country houses, staring across acres of fresh green lawns. He was arm-in-arm with someone whose name he could not remember. There were trees, birds, flowers. He slept in rooms with monogrammed pillows. Someone was talking about cricket, rugby. He was standing up and making another speech. 'The youth of this country could be a volunteer force for the army.' There were squawking ravens, oak trees, pheasants, peacocks. He was gazing into a mirror examining himself to see if he had yet become a god.

(And in the midst of this his guilt, his guilt. Christine must remain free from this adulation; she knew different. She would hate it, he told himself, but was that not a lie? At the very heart of him this lie. And sometimes her meekness, sometimes her recriminations. And the biggest truth of all, that he didn't love her, that he was not capable of the love she demanded.)

He walked in and out of castles to music. Sometimes he slept and sometimes he didn't. And at times the speeches were immensely boring, and he still had to smile. He reached into these deep recesses of himself for that smile; it was worse to summon up than courage. He had to listen to stories, narratives, invented fictions from his past. They made him and remade him and he had no say in their product.

And from this to Dingwall, gay with flags and flowers. The famous Omdurman cannon was decked with evergreen, and above it waved the flag captured by himself from the Dervishes. There were pipes: cannon belched as he drove up to the square and jumped to the ground. He wore a bright scarlet tunic, the front of which was breastplated with stars and orders. He was presented with the Freedom of the Burgh by Provost Stewart, a boyhood friend, who made a long speech. And an address of welcome and another scroll of honour.

No one could defeat him now. With such a number of swords he must be invulnerable! But he felt more comfortable here than in London. The surrounding hills were a true memory among so many who claimed to have been his boyhood friend, in that dream, in that exhausted dream. 'It was here that I learned what integrity and assiduity I have . . . ' And the faces looking at him. If only he were witty, spontaneous, brilliant. But no, he must not be that. Still, these faces were different from the London faces, uncomplicated by ambition, not proud. And the men wore caps and homespun and held their caps in their hands while he spoke. But for fate he might have been one of them, gentle, slightly uncomprehending, in that rain.

Then Tain and Inverness. And a welcome arranged for him outside the old schoolhouse at Mulbuie, in the soft Highland rain, himself, to everyone's disappointment, dressed in mufti which didn't quite fit him. The schoolmaster, old Mr Treasurer, speaking in Gaelic, and someone holding an umbrella above his own head in the incessant rain.

And old Mr Treasurer of course knew that he would come to something, that he wasn't ordinary. Beside that hut which looked almost like one he had seen somewhere else and which he was attacking with his sword raised. And he said that he owed much of what he had done to trembling, Gaelic-speaking old Mr Treasurer.

And talking to Mr Treasurer, rather frail now, as to a stranger among the cool rain and the mountains. It was as if it wasn't him they were talking about. Let me put my hand in yours, old man, you are real, this schoolhouse is real; I could cry but I am not allowed to cry, the statue is not allowed to cry. That Mr Treasurer should change so much, that this schoolhouse should exist. And it was as if the narrations were about someone else, someone he had long forgotten about.

That night he had a dream. In the dream was a crocodile which was lying cagily in mud. The crocodile snapped upwards at him, and the blue and white birds flew above it. He saw the teeth opening like walls, and the birds were sucked down that long fetid tunnel. I will not have that, he thought, and went for a gun, but the bullets bounced off the crocodile hide, which was thick and reptilian, and the crocodile had a cold green eye.

The crocodile was changed into a man who was standing on a street. The man's finger pointed at him. I need you, it said.

Can I bear this weight, he thought, this weight of adulation? I am not clever, I am not eloquent, I am a simple soldier. I didn't want that green unsleeping eye. This being that they have created will eat me up if I am not careful.

And all the while Mr Treasurer spoke in Gaelic through a high wind.

And men with their caps in their hands looked at him, but innocently and without malice.

And later, in June, Hector was made an LLD at Glasgow University and stood outside the ancient building on a lawn, talking. And it was stranger than anything else to be in this place. As if he were an academic (though of course he knew Urdu and Arabic). What could he say to these quiet men who flourished in inaction? The dream was continuing and becoming even stranger. 'I foresee a day when . . . ' The words came out of the mouth of the statue, while summer blazed around it. And they were all quiet – for him. Bald, inactive men were listening to him. And one of the latter gazed up at him, 'What is it like . . . I mean . . . to kill a man?' And for a moment they gazed into each other's eyes as if they knew each other to the bone. The Dervishes, he thought absurdly, will never capture Glasgow University. And he looked over at the invited audience sipping their sherries, eating their tiny morsels of food.

And the exhausting, perplexing dream. And in the trees he heard the voices of ravens. And it took him all his time to keep his stone foot planted on the lawn as the hooded photographers snapped.

It was all so different from the army where the life was fixed. But in the dream he moved among peasants and professors, among elegant swords and rain, among peering and respectful faces. He was the myth, the legend, fallen upon and eaten. And he felt so tired, so tired, as if his fate were that of the victim, not that of the victor. He lived among flags, flowers, speeches.

His hand was sore with shaking hands. At night he looked out at the unattainable desert moon. Perhaps he had been too long away, too much a hermit who governed obedient men.

'Would you care to have a look at this . . . '

'As a matter of fact I have a little gun here . . . '

'Curiously enough I was thinking of an incident . . . '

'I suppose it must be a strange sensation to face an enemy force . . . ?'

'I don't suppose you remember me . . . '

'I'm sure you'll have forgotten all your Gaelic . . . '

'In my early days I was in the Sudan myself . . . '

'Is it really as hot as they say . . . ?'

(If there was someone with me I could talk to. I cannot talk to Christine. And why in any case should she talk to me? She has been better to me than I have been to her. But my nature . . . No, I cannot talk to her. And in any case the army has betrayed her.)

And in Aberdeen, where he visited the barracks and met some of his old sergeants and sergeant-majors, he met Alister Robertson, son of a doctor, who attended a public school where he had lectured.

Hector fell in love – absolutely, unpredictably – with his uniform, his perfected beauty, his momentary becalmed loveliness. Love burned in him for the unattainable boy, a pain which he had not felt before, and of which he did not know he was capable. For that young, negligent, aloof Adonis, as for someone he perplexedly might have known, might have been – unproblematic, confident of self, assured. A kind of alternative being which might have been a possibility. And yet not simply a self, for how could he with such passion, such pain, love himself, and not the one uniformed as he himself was, not of the slovenly civilian kind?

So that he began to write letters to him, biting his tongue to appear reasonable, though affectionate. For he must not frighten off that eternal boy who, disciplined by school set among rich green acres, was not a clumsy lout in tackety boots setting off for a mean hut on a frosty day.

He burned as with the untreated malaria which sometimes

shook him, ageing, exhausted, overdone by speeches, politeness, requests, invitations. The man, old beyond his years, gazed out stunned at the flawless boy, cap tilted on head, cheeks red and blossoming.

He wrote letters to him in his lonely nights, when freed of the day's turmoil, tongue-tied in his ill-fitting suit. Father he was, protector, shield, so that bodies, daggers, blood, might not hurt Alister. At all costs he must be protected from swords and guns, and from the women who stabbed in the snow.

So that the Dervishes might not enfold him in their cloudy skirts. So that age might not have him, nor domesticity, nor the slovenly untidinesses of the day. So that the flies might not eat him nor the sand engulf him.

And his letters were commentary, report from the streaming world in which he lived, was tossed, almost drowned, though the smile held on, fixed like a rictus.

So that gravity might not have him. Nor the women with their viperish tongues. Nor the night towards which he returned, exhausted and insomniac.

The marvellous boy was a fixed portrait from reality to whom he was hero, though he walked like a shambling peasant in a dream.

11

To HECTOR'S chagrin, instead of being assigned to a command in South Africa where war had been renewed, he was appointed to the Sirkind District in India with the local rank of brigadier-general.

On the voyage out he couldn't but think of his first journey to India many years before, and the happy, intense years he had spent there in a much more negligent youth. Now it was different. He dreaded a peacetime command: he felt tired and often depressed, and he missed Alister.

Sometimes, however, he would note the people he met on the ship so that he might write about them later to Alister: and also the sights he saw, the birds that flew about the ship, the natives seen at various ports. Sometimes as he watched the water flashing past, he saw perfectly reflected in it the innocent flawless face of his loved one. Later he would write to him of elephants, of huts made of leaves, of parakeets and monkeys, bullocks, camels, torrential rivers.

But the camp itself and his short time there was a continuous nightmare. He was suffering from malaria and diarrhoea. He was expected to entertain but though he was given an allowance it was not enough. He dreaded the chit-chat, the barbed comments of the women. He knew that they imitated his almost incomprehensible accent behind his back. Their quick, glittering sharpnesses were abhorrent to him. He tried to remain equable and cheerful but he found it almost impossible.

The camp hung from his will but he had to drag himself out of bed in the mornings. He was a wounded giant, an Ajax. War was much simpler than this. Instead of the sound of guns there was the click-clack of intrigues, scenarios of rank and precedence, injured egos.

He became short-tempered, snapping at officers who had come to India to enjoy themselves, for leave for them was plentiful, and even for the men there were no menial duties. The officers' picture of India was one of well-trained silent servants, games of polo, tennis, the club visited for a peg in the evening, expeditions for tiger, pig-sticking, the pursuit of jackals with hounds, races.

And now there was this vast shadow cast over the camp, this being who would interrogate them on drill, who would sometimes make them take over from the sergeants. He was a curious, melancholy, demanding Scotsman. They had heard too that he had won fame by commanding nig-nogs.

Hector was bored by the monotony of the life, by the social superfluities. Sometimes during a rare dinner party he might almost fall asleep. He wanted in his phantom rages to strike out at these people, almost as if they were worse than Dervishes. He had to be careful not to submit to idleness, not to be eaten up by laziness. He would hear the noises made by the punkah as in a dream. And there was always the chit-chat of the women, embroidering reputations.

The diarrhoea itself weakened him: it seemed a steady diminution of his self, a new wateriness, as if he was under the rays of the planet Pisces. It was part of his helplessness and his confusion. It was a sign of approaching autumn: he had spent himself recklessly and now he was paying the price.

This then was also part of the Empire, this vacuum. He needed to have someone at his side, someone who could deal with these wives, someone inured by class to deal with these matters to which he was not accustomed. He hated the idleness; he was like a sad bullock prodded by negligent drivers. He mooned about and then would suddenly snap and snarl.

He would sit in the club for hours playing soldiers with matches, setting up companies, battalions, trying out manoeuvres.

And then, as to a prisoner, there came the order of release: he was to go to South Africa to a military command again. (There had been dramatic reverses there for the British army.)

The shadow lifted from the camp: he was buoyant, purposeful, cheerful. Air entered the barracks as if great windows had been opened. But he was not forgiven: he was like a black dream they had dreamed. Let him take his bleak Scottish loneliness elsewhere, let him wage war with his matches on some foreign field. This unnatural, fidgety presence was being removed: and everyone rejoiced.

He was to return to South Africa with Roberts and Kitchener. The war heroes were being sent for in that dark hour when the sharpshooters of the Old Testament took on the Empire again.

Everywhere there was disaster: at Ladysmith, at Kimberley, at Mafeking. Lord Methuen had ordered the Highland Brigade at Magersfontein to carry out a frontal attack on a night of rain and bitter cold on the Boer entrenchments. 'Your first duty,' he had told them, 'is to the Queen, the next to your country and lastly to yourselves.' Whereupon he quoted to the Highland Brigade from Henry V's speech delivered before Agincourt.

Yet in that strange Agincourt, what Lord Methuen did not appear to have known was that he was faced by trenches on both sides of the Modder River, and by a barrier of barbed wire manned by sharpshooters. When the first Highland soldier stumbled, as well he might at this sharp unknown trap, accidentally setting off his rifle, the area was flooded with searchlights in which the Highland Brigade – Argylls, Seaforths, Black Watch and Highland Light Infantry – were clearly delineated and then annihilated. The Highland Brigade broke in disorder and panic. Lord Methuen never forgave them for refusing to clamber helplessly through barbed wire without wire-cutters in the face of a killing fire. 'Cowards!' he shouted at them, in the ruined shadow of his lost Agincourt.

And so calls went out for previous victors, Lord Roberts as Commander-in-Chief, Lord Kitchener as his Chief of Staff, and Hector Macdonald to take command of the demoralised Highland Brigade which had been led by the now dead Wauchope, a friend and admirer of Hector's from Omdurman days.

But, as Hector knew, the Boer was far more formidable than

the Afghan or the Dervish; he had the capacity for sustained and continued action, subtly controlled and orchestrated.

Still, this trio, of whom Hector was one, would soon put a stop to them. Hector arrived in Capetown from India in the third week of January and left on the 21st for the Modder River. On 3 February, with the Highland Brigade – all that was left of them – the 9th Lancers and a battery of Field Artillery, he left Lord Methuen's camp for Koodosberg Drift, fourteen miles to the west.

Hector considered that his first task in the short time available to him was to restore confidence to his Brigade. He talked to his sergeant-majors and built up a picture of what had happened both before the Brigade had entered battle and after; this was what he learned.

In the march under Lord Methuen the British soldiers had no tents, though the days were torridly hot and the nights bitterly cold. The Boers waited for them on the kopjes, picking them off with accurate rifle-fire and then retreating to distant kopjes. At Belmont and Enslin, between 100 and 200 were killed or wounded in this way, while the Boers drifted away on horseback. General Cronje had ditches dug on the south side of the river, and positioned a screen of his men there. On the north side there were more ditches protected by the main force.

On a sunny morning the British soldiers were marching negligently along, smoking their pipes, talking, laughing, when they were devastated by a sudden fire. All that day they lay in the hot sun, thirsty, hungry, and at the end of the day the Boers were still entrenched in their ditches. It seemed that they would be fighting again the next day, but in the darkness of the night the Boers unaccountably vanished. Had the British won after all? No, Cronje had merely retreated to a stronger position, a line of hills called Magersfontein. Lord Methuen had already had 1,000 men wounded or killed.

It was at this point at the Modder River that the Highland Brigade joined them.

Shell after shell was thrown across the river but there was no movement from the Boers. Lord Methuen decided, without true

112

knowledge of what was happening, to make an assault in the darkness of the night. On the Sunday therefore the Brigade made its advance. There was heavy rain, and at a distance of three miles from the hills the men lay down on the wet ground, one blanket between two men. At one in the morning they made their way forward, hungry and wet, in close formation. The Black Watch went first, then the Seaforths, then the Argylls and the HLI. Methuen thought that the Boers were on the hills, but they were on the plain in front, in deep trenches protected by barbed wire.

'That was the worst, sir,' the NCOs said, 'the barbed wire. You see, sir, we had no cutters. When we went into the barbed wire, some of the soldiers shouted at the shock, and the Boers began to fire. We were in close formation, sir, and one bullet went through six men.

'There were 4,000 men in the brigade. In five minutes 600 were dead, among them Brigadier Wauchope. It was then that we broke, sir, though we re-formed later.'

'Never mind,' said Hector quietly, 'the same happened to me at Majuba.'

He left the NCOs and talked to the men, finding out their names and where they came from. He seemed massively tranquil. He assured them that there would be a fresh start. Inwardly he seethed, thinking of Wauchope dead. These damned murderous Boers.

But again, in spite of his own tiredness, he must be the Hector Macdonald of the myth: they were looking to him as if he would save them. He was the eternal legend though no longer Fighting Mac, now Old Mac.

He wrote to Alister:

Many thanks for the photographs, which I like very much. Can you guess why I like the small one best? I am sending you a tin of the Queen's chocolate, which you can eat with your best friends and think of me. You should keep the tin as a memento. And now for a lecture for not giving me more news in detail. News, news, news! to please me – all about your own dear self.

113

He addressed the troops, telling them about his complete confidence in them, about the traditions of Highland regiments. He said that the people at home would be waiting for good news of them.

And so he led them to Paardeburg, which was fought at first under Kitchener, as Roberts was sick. The Brigade marched thirty-one miles in twenty-four hours, each man carrying 100 rounds of ammunition, greatcoat, cholera belt, one day's rations, bottle of water, waterproof sheet and blanket, the whole weighing something like sixty pounds.

Kitchener made his usual frontal attack on the Boer laager. This time the assault was in the daytime, not in the dark, but the result was the same. Hector, who was under Kitchener's orders, guided his brigade across bare, open, unsheltered ground exposed to withering fire from the Boers. The wounded lay in the hot sun without shelter or water. The accuracy of the enemy fire was as usual astonishing and devastating. Hector himself was wounded in the foot and his horse killed. He was taken unwillingly to hospital. His fury against the Boers was intense. How could such an army win such continual victories? How could amateurs defeat professionals? He was angry with himself, with Methuen, with Kitchener. His dogma of discipline and drill was disintegrating in this accursed country, in the face of these negligent farmers who drifted like will-o'-the-wisps about South Africa. This was a new kind of warfare to which he had difficulty adapting himself. Did it demand more discipline or less? He burned with helpless rage, so much so that he didn't at times feel the pain in his foot. He wanted out of the hospital to fight again. This time, this time . . . His body felt heavy, mortal, shadowy. It was as if he was beginning to sense a gradual disintegration, an autumn fading. His leg throbbed dully. But surely if he was given another chance . . . This land was ill luck and disaster for him. Here some kind of bleak star shone on him. First Majuba, then this. He asked continually for news. Roberts had taken over and shelled Cronje out of his laager. Cronje was in a death-trap. Hector wrote to Roberts reminding him of the anniversary of Majuba. Let the surrender wait till then. And this was done.

He got up from his bed and returned to his Brigade. Outside

Bloemfontein he nearly fainted. He rode ahead of his marching troops, his wound throbbing. The army spent six weeks at Bloemfontein, for it was plagued by shortages, and tired horses, and typhoid. In the heat of the day the men had been drinking water from the Modder River, polluted by detritus from Cronje's camp. In one day fifty men died. There were 1,000 fresh graves in the cemetery.

In April Roberts left Bloemfontein, glad to be rid of the plaguey bodies, the endless burying. He was heading for Pretoria. Now the rains were over, the sky was blue, the earth green. The soldiers whistled and sang. Roberts, on horseback, sat for an hour watching his army march past. He seemed to have shrivelled and grown old: his only son had been killed at Colenso. It seemed that the war was over except that the Boers resorted to guerrilla warfare, cutting the railroads again and again. The Highland Brigade was disbanded and given the task of guarding the railway.

To this, Hector, disenchanted and wounded, had come. He was being eased down a siding away from the central thrust of the war. He was like a chugging old train carried along by its own momentum. The predestined rails glittered. To this he had finally come. This was a new war to be fought in new ways. He was becoming an anachronism, tired and humiliated, with a throbbing foot. Even that had become comic. He wrote to his brother William forbidding him to speak to the Press. He had noticed in a newspaper a garbled report of his wound, 'purporting to have been given by you. Of course I know such was not supplied by you. But in case of accident I want you to remember what I wrote to you some years since, not to give any information concerning me to the newspapers. Do please try to bear this in mind.'

There were comic reports of his wound.

MACDONALD'S WOUND

Monday morning: Macdonald only received a single wound but being in the ankle it is painful.

Monday midday: Macdonald's single wound is not troublesome as it is only in the little finger.

115

Monday evening: Macdonald's single wound, being in the lungs, causes much anxiety.

Tuesday morning: Macdonald's single wound – in the hip – is doing well.

Tuesday mid-day: Macdonald's single wound – which penetrates the brain and liver and ends at the great toe – is somewhat painful.

Tuesday evening: Macdonald's single wound causes no uneasiness, as it is only in the haversack.

As his gaze travelled the tracks searching for Boers he felt himself to be an ancient posthumous figure, destroyed by this phantom army of snipers, rusty as some of the rails were, slowly chugging towards a minor station.

He had strange ideas. Why not tempt the Boer children with sweets to tell the whereabouts of their fathers who were tormenting him? And he wrote to the *St James' Gazette* advocating conscription:

I should take the period for service just after a man has finished his apprenticeship, or been a short time a journeyman, but not yet settled down. A year or two at that period, in an age ranging from twenty-one to twenty-three, would not I am convinced injure one's prospects if passed in a well-regulated army, and a well-regulated army a conscript army is bound to be.

He himself of course had run away to the army before finishing his apprenticeship. It seemed centuries ago.

It seemed odd that he himself should be writing to the newspapers after telling his brother William not to.

Words, words, he told himself disgustedly, feeling the throb in his foot like a diseased engine.

This bloody country where the enemy swarmed like flies and you couldn't hit them. This bloody vicious country inhabited by an invisible enemy. It was even worse than Afghanistan with its criss-cross rivers, its heat and cold, its fevers, dysentery, typhoid, pneumonia, and the Boer who, unlike the Dervish, did not leap towards death as towards heaven. No, the Boer would live if he could. His heaven, though real enough, could wait for a while yet.

Put in command of a column of yeomanry – volunteer cavalry of upper-class Englishmen – Hector, whose main love was the regular army, would flash out at them with barely concealed rage. Once he told them that he would put them off their horses and instal Highland infantry in the saddles instead.

Another time, after a long march, he furiously harangued some volunteer infantry, saying that they were dirty, and ordering them to polish their buttons: all this when these soldiers, like the regulars, suffered as in the Sudan, hot days, cold nights, dust, flies, infection and disease, locusts, and of course the Boers.

It was as if he wished to retain a system of strict regulations which was no longer appropriate to a changing warfare. He was, however, delighted when he met the Lovat Scouts, a Highland volunteer regiment raised by Lord Lovat and intended to be a species of spies to find out where the Boers in fact were, since often they were invisible, as they had been to Lord Methuen. Organised from shepherds and gamekeepers, and briefly trained, they were sent to South Africa where they also helped to defend the railway.

To them of course Hector would speak in Gaelic, and at that time he was happier speaking to ordinary soldiers than to officers.

Sometimes too he would expatiate on the conduct of the war, blaming the quality of the Lee Enfield Rifle, among other things. His leg troubled him, but what troubled him most was his isolation from the centre of the war.

When Kitchener established his concentration camps and burned down Boer farms and crops, and 'like wild animals' herded the Boers into enclosures, 'like Greek or Italian bandits', Hector and his men had to guard a camp on the Orange River which, like most of the other camps, was squalid and disgusting.

One of his sergeants said to Hector, 'It's an awful thing to be fighting such God-fearing people.' Nor was the comparison with Cumberland lost on him.

He used his power to protect some of the Boers' cattle, and did not see much point in burning their farms; burning their crops would have been enough. Having grown up in the Highlands he knew about cattle and crops, and would, whenever he could, talk to the Boers and try to help them. He found them religious like the Highlanders, honest and kind. As refugees swirled helplessly about him, he felt that this was not a way to conduct a war. There had been no attempt to provide food or shelter for these people, stunned by their dispersal from their homes. Women and children wandered about in a daze, hungry and without accommodation. They would come to him for help and advice. The more he saw of them the more he liked them. They had a bluff integrity which appealed to him. Seen close to, they were not the demons of his imagination. They were sufferers like himself. He too sometimes felt like a refugee and in his tent, bare except for an oriental curtain, would hold forth, perhaps not wisely, on the war. He spent time with the privates. He felt that he had been dispossessed by the new leadership. Was this a job for a soldier, to be guarding women and children in a camp?

In April 1901 he was relieved, by Kitchener, of his command, and sent home. He returned to London on the *Carisbrooke Castle*, and was knighted by King Edward VII on 14 May. A week later he was off to India to take up the command of the Southern District army at Belgaum.

He had been rewarded for his service in South Africa but felt within himself that he was not the Hector, the Fighting Mac, he had once been. He still felt tired and bewildered by his spell in South Africa. Something was sliding away from him: some power that he had once had at a time and in a place that had suited his soldier's personality. The Boer war had injured him profoundly at the centre of his being. His wound had sapped him. He felt that a new generation of officers was taking over and that he was simply Old Mac. Simple heroism could no longer serve. Perhaps discipline itself was no longer enough, nor a constellation of brightly polished buttons. And now he was to return again to the loneliness of India.

12

WHEN he arrived in Madras to take up his appointment at Belgaum, Hector felt that his future there could not be faced without some rest, and asked for the three months' leave he had given up to come to India. It was decided that he should go on an official visit to Australia and New Zealand, in order in fact to propagandise for the Empire among these dominions when help was needed (as had happened in South Africa).

Restored to a fairly central role among people of whom many were Scottish in origin, Hector enjoyed his tour, and was, as after the Sudan, flattered and revered. He became more fluent and easy in his speech-making. He spoke in Melbourne and Adelaide. He advocated his system of military service. Boys at school would do some military training, and later, at the age of twenty-two, would enlist for a period of six months to a year. As if still clinging to an illusionary system that had failed, he repeated that discipline and drill were the most important virtues as far as the making of a soldier were concerned.

He spoke lyrically of 'clean-limbed' schoolboys, recalling Alister to whom he still wrote. Young cadets preparing to defend their country dominated his imagination.

He was unaware of stirrings in Australia that were not Imperialistic. For instance, the editor of *The Boomerang* had written in 1891:

This is no time for airy persiflage: brutal frankness is the one thing appropriate to the occasion. Australia is a democracy: Australians are democrats, and the scheme which would drag this nascent nation at the heels of an antipodal monarch is rank treason to the noblest Australian ideals. The Imperialistic sentiment to which Sir Henry Parker gives such ardent expression when he 'prays God that Australia may remain under the British flag', the sentiment which impels servile political and society leaders to pay such slavish adulation to gubernatorial figure-heads and to scorn no path, however degrading, which may lead them into the direct or reflected sunshine of the royal favour, has no place in the minds of native-born Australians . . . Both instinct and reason prompt a contempt for the fetish of hereditary royalty . . .

Hector, however, did not know this: nor had he much time to read newspapers or magazines. He had an idealistic and simplistic view of the Commonwealth. As in South Africa, Australia was trying to define itself, and to calculate its destiny. Melbourne was compared to London but more precisely to New York. The Australian was a new type, individualistic, irreverent, not particularly scholarly.

Still, Hector made his speeches, was known, recognised from his photographs, but also appeared less military-looking and more light-hearted than had been expected. 'A sturdy, thick-set, cheery-looking man, scarcely middle-aged . . . in a brown slouch hat, soft shirt, and a blue suit . . . ' He looked like a 'station overseer' or a 'good-natured contractor'.

Still immersed in his dream of Empire, still believing in 'drill and discipline', Hector travelled through Australia and New Zealand, bringing out to hear him those especially of Scots descent, unaware in Australia of a young nation testing out its own identity: until his three months were over and he had to return to India, only to discover that he had been sent to Ceylon instead, as he had been pleading with Roberts in London to do for some time.

Hector had been impressed by Australia and, of course, by Melbourne, with its long wide streets, its banks, shops, warehouses, cathedrals, churches, parliament house, hospital, library, jewellers' stores and so on.

He had been flattered to read in *The Times* that he should

be offered the post of Commander-in-Chief of the Australian army.

After the comparative débâcle of South Africa, he had been listened to, and with deference. He had of course been unaware of the rise of trade unionism and Labour in Australia. Nor had he read criticisms of the 'banality' of Melbourne and the attacks on fine old English gentlemen who on the hottest days dressed buttoned up in blue and drab and black and drank their decanters of port with absurd dignity.

The Australians too were competing for the destinies of their young. Some thought that they had a grievous dislike of mental effort. Some were sure that they ignored art and literature and should be holding debates and having elocution lessons to prepare themselves for the important work that they would have to do when the destinies of the southern continent passed into their hands.

Hector was only one man – and an outsider – competing for the Australian youth. He left convinced that he had been successful on his tour. The land of phantom gum trees, and strange, eerie animals and birds, gazed back at him. He had been there for far too short a time to understand its aboriginal oddnesses, and its varied strivings towards self.

Ceylon was not the haven Hector had expected. It was rigidly stratified, with an elite of tea planters' families and English civil servant brahmins. The planters lived in the Highlands in bungalows with gardens in which roses grew as in England, while the civil servants moved in exclusive clubs and hotels in Colombo. The planters, regarded as ignorant 'white sahibs' by the native Sinhalese and Tamils, led a happy and pleasant existence. They had every kind of reasonable relaxation – tennis courts, squash courts, cricket nets and swimming pools. Their clubs were exclusive to whites, and on Saturday evenings there were dances. There was no social intercourse between the whites and the coloureds.

Hector was asked to the planters' houses, but did not wish to go. Their interests were not his, and he was not 'one of them'. For their part they soon recognised this. He could have held dinners, as Kitchener did in India, since he now had a reasonable salary, but he felt uncomfortable in that codified world.

There wasn't very much for him to do, and the army was small. There was no military threat to Ceylon. He had time on his hands which he spent drilling his troops.

There was a Ceylon militia officered by planters, with the Governor, Sir Joseph Ridgeway, as its Colonel-in-Chief. Ridgeway had been in Afghanistan when Hector had been there and had served as political secretary to General Roberts. He had taken part in the Kandahar expedition. Hector, invited to inspect the militia, put them through their paces as if they were regulars, and shouted at the officers. He was determined to show that in his own field he was knowledgeable and expert. However, he came across as a harsh, abrasive sergeant. On that beautiful island to which Adam and Eve were supposed to have come after being ejected from Paradise, he appeared as a rough, irascible presence.

He felt unhappy and miserable in a world he did not really understand and did not fit into. As in India, he knew that he was being talked about and probably mocked. He felt like a Tamil himself, an outsider. He had no interest in the sports the planters engaged in, though of course at one time he had played football.

More and more it became clear to him that he was not a peacetime soldier and that without the element of war he was inadequate and almost unreal.

Also sometimes he did not feel well and would break out into inexplicable rages. There was no opening for him into that fixed world, which he felt to be alien and hostile. He tried to talk to Ridgeway but Ridgeway always seemed to be busy with his schemes for extending railways, setting up an irrigation department, supervising the creation of a university for Ceylon. And also he had been offended by Hector's curious unprofessional outburst.

Where have I found myself? thought Hector. In this calm island, settled by self-satisfied planters and civil servants, what am I to do? He felt superfluous. How could he use his abilities here? Sometimes he felt like the stone lion which had been built at Sigiriya, wishing for a violence he could contend with. But there was no violence. The days of Ceylon's murders, parricides, internecine battles were over.

He made friends with some of the burgher families, old Ceylonese families, often Portuguese, who had married into native families. They formed the professional classes – lawyers, bankers, etc. – but they did not belong to the rarefied upper echelons of the island. Among them he felt comfortable, and especially with the de Saram family who had two young boys. He would give the boys presents and tell them about India, the Sudan and his various military exploits. He found them polite and handsome. They reminded him of Alister.

De Saram himself told him some of the history of Ceylon, about the period when the Portuguese had ruled the island, before the Dutch and British, when Portugal had been an ancient and proud empire. He had read about the early lion ancestors of Ceylon, demon princes and princesses, stupas and temples. De Saram was a Roman Catholic among Protestants, Buddhists and Hindus. He resented the icy attitudes of the British.

Hector took the boys on expeditions, to the beaches, to the Highlands. They listened as he told them about the Dervishes and the Boers. He rehearsed his life with them and felt comfortable. He felt their aura of a future as his own world was fading. Their mannerly beauty appealed to him. He took them to a festival at Kandy which was held by torchlight, with caparisoned elephants, drummers and dancers, chieftains in jewelled costumes, and whip-crackers.

They made no demands on him, they accepted him, he did not feel vulnerable with them. He was with them a great deal: he sometimes played football with them. They refreshed him in his constricted life. He did not care what the Brahmins or the planters thought.

He felt a kind of recklessness, as if defences which he had created over the years were beginning to crack. He wished to stretch out for human contact, beyond the armour he had perfected. He would sometimes absent-mindedly stroke the boys' hair, touch them, as with the despair of a dying man. On the edge of this world he could hear biting words, laughter. He would go on railway expeditions of his own.

I have no place, he thought, that is what is wrong. I have no place.

And also he had acute sexual urges for which there was no outlet. These he had once controlled, but now they were beating against his armour, in this climate – outwardly serene – of his fading days.

When Hector was announced at Nuwara Eiya, the Governor's summer residence in the hills, Ridgeway was standing at the large window looking out. He turned immediately and said, 'Sir Hector, how kind of you. Would you like to sit down? Whisky?'

'Please.'

Silently, Ridgeway poured out whiskies for the two of them, handed a glass to Hector, but remained standing. He seemed to have something to say but to have difficulty in saying it. Finally, he said, 'Sir Hector, I have asked you to come here for a special reason. It's a very delicate matter.'

Hector looked at him inquiringly.

'It's really . . . Well, first of all, you have been very friendly with the de Saram family. That is correct, is it?'

'Yes, sir,' said Hector. He sipped the whisky, though he wanted to drink it in one gulp.

'And with their two sons?'

'Yes, sir.'

'I see. Well, rumours have been going round the island, though perhaps they have not reached you. Rumours that you are over-friendly with them. You give them presents?'

'I have done.'

'Expensive ones?'

'Reasonably.'

'These rumours suggest that your relationship with them goes beyond the bounds of friendship.'

There was a silence in the room.

'What are you suggesting, sir?'

'These are not only suggestions, Sir Hector. I am afraid there is more. A planter says he saw you with four native schoolboys in a railway carriage. But more serious than that, two Anglican clergymen say that they saw you in a railway carriage with about seventy schoolboys. The suggestion is that . . . '

Again he paused, as if he had difficulty in speaking.

'The suggestion is that . . . something improper was going on. Furthermore, the clergymen say that they are willing to testify to this, and so are the schoolboys . . . ' He began to speak more quickly. 'The local newspapers have heard of these rumours but I have asked them to keep quiet about it for the moment. Till something is done. Have you anything to say?'

Hector looked up at him like a bull that had been struck. He spoke after a long pause.

'You say that these clergymen and the schoolboys are willing to testify to whatever they say they saw?'

'I'm afraid so.'

'I see. Then it won't really matter if I say I was innocent of whatever they accuse me of.'

'What do you mean?'

'Those in important positions on the island do not greatly care for me, and if there are two clergymen, as you say, sir—'

'But, man, are you innocent or not of this . . . improper behaviour?'

'I think that is not the point, sir. It is possible that this is a way of getting at me. I have of course not been popular here.'

'Surely you aren't suggesting that such a large number of schoolboys and two clergymen are involved in a conspiracy against you?'

'I have not been popular,' Hector repeated stubbornly. 'As to the presents to the de Saram children—'

'That is the least of it, Sir Hector. I am sure you will agree that this has been a very difficult interview for me. We both know that such . . . such practices are not a civil offence on this island, but in the case of a man in a responsible position such as yourself they are very grave. It falls to me as your superior to deal with the problem. As you point out yourself, a rumour in such a case is almost as bad as a conviction, especially with so many witnesses. I may not

125

be able to prevent the newspapers from referring to them much longer.'

'I was always friendly with newspapers,' said Hector in a quiet voice.

'What did you say?'

'Nothing, sir. I was thinking aloud. Perhaps I brought this on myself by cultivating the burghers rather than the planters.'

'I don't think that is relevant, Sir Hector. Either you are innocent or not. If you are innocent, you will have to say so.'

'I doubt if that would suffice, sir, with all due respect.'

'I see.'

There was another long silence while Ridgeway paced up and down.

'I am afraid that the clergymen are persistent, Sir Hector, as they feel it to be their duty. I am very vexed at this. There is so much to be done on the island and so little time to do it.' He became brisker. 'I have been pondering this situation for some time and I have a suggestion to make. I shall contact Lord Roberts in London and suggest that you be given leave. That will give time for you to be given another posting if that is what Lord Roberts decides. On balance I think that might be the best immediate solution. Of course you might wish to stay here and face things out. What do you wish to do?'

'I should prefer to accept your first suggestion, sir.'

'Are you sure?'

'Yes, I am sure.'

'Good. Then I will inform Lord Roberts of the situation. I need hardly say that I have found this very delicate, very difficult. You have of course served under Lord Roberts?'

'Yes, sir, in Afghanistan and South Africa.'

'Of course . . . I . . . I sincerely hope a solution will be found.'

Hector got to his feet and stood for a moment as if at attention. 'Thank you, sir.'

'No, no . . . you have nothing to thank me for . . .' He made as if to hold out his hand, but didn't do so.

'That is all then, Sir Hector. You will need to prepare yourself.

When Hector had gone, Lady Ridgeway, a woman of great beauty, came into the room.

'Has he gone, Joseph?'

'Yes, poor devil. I'm sorry for him.'

'But such an unnatural—'

'I . . . we must be charitable. He was very lonely. He didn't fit in here. This is the most unpleasant task I have ever had to perform. The man was a first-rate soldier. He rose from the ranks, you know.'

'Nevertheless—'

'And then again, he spent a great deal of his service among the Arabs. It is not a good thing to be a bachelor. I don't think it has hit him yet. His whole career . . . Poor devil, poor devil.'

Before taking ship to England, Hector was interviewed by the *Ceylon Observer* by whom he was asked why he was departing so suddenly. He answered, smiling, 'I have been asked to go to London, and I am taking advantage of the SS *Ophir* being in Colombo to go there immediately.'

'Are you being given other special duties and further promotion, perhaps?'

'You want to know that, do you? Of course I can't tell you that. I'm surprised that you found out so quickly that I was leaving the island for a while. You must have a very good intelligence service.'

'Oh, we have, sir.'

'Well, I am very sorry to go, but I may come back soon, eh?' He smiled and the reporter smiled.

In the harbour, the SS *Ophir* waited.

On board there were a number of Scots who came up and spoke to Hector. He seemed jovial and happy as if he was glad to be leaving the island, though he did not say so. The secret hierarchical codes of Ceylon vanished into the blue waters of the sea. But he also knew that there were some on the ship who knew that he had not been popular on the island. The relief of leaving the 'jewel of the sea' was tremendous, however, and his spirits lifted as the ship made progress towards first Port Said and then Naples. He slept dreamlessly, as if an immense tiredness had lifted from him. The sea voyage seemed for the moment at least to insulate him against rancour and regret as if he were floating free of consequences, while some of the Scots talked to him about

127

Omdurman and he for his part relived part of his past life, distant and intact and with a separate purity of its own.

When the ship docked at Port Said he was befriended by a Gaelic-speaking minister, the Rev. Dr J. K. Campbell, who said to him in Gaelic, 'Bha mi bruidhinn ri feadhainn air an t-soitheach agus chan eil iad cho cairdeil's a tha thu smaoineachadh (I was speaking to some people on the ship, and they are not so friendly as you think).' Hector spoke to him in Gaelic too. Speaking their own intimate language, they had their own secret code. The minister sensed in Hector a strange brittle gaiety which disturbed him. Later on, however, he suddenly said, 'It might have been better if I had never left the Highlands.' And, 'There's more to the army than soldiering.'

'God will keep us all,' said the minister. 'Perhaps we should pray more often than we do.'

Hector mentioned Buddhism which he had come across on the island. He also said that he found the English difficult to talk to, and that he was glad to be speaking some Gaelic again. He told Campbell that he had a brother still in Rootfield on the Black Isle, but often seemed restless as if there was something on his mind.

'I don't suppose I shall visit him this time,' he said. He talked about the Puritanical nature of the Highlanders. Then he said, 'We are born to live certain lives and we can't change anything.'

Once they were standing at the rail and Hector pointed to the early-rising moon. 'That is the same moon as shines over the Black Isle. I have always been a wanderer. Even when I was young. My father was a mason and I used to travel with him. I regret that I joined the army without telling him. But in those days nothing else would do.'

'Do you have regrets, then?' said the minister.

'About the soldiering, no. A man must be what he is.' He looked down at the wake as if it reminded him of fate and predestination.

'I used to talk to the Arabs. They believe in predestination. I loved them. That was the most satisfying period of my life. They had a childish faith.'

The two of them parted at Naples.

'Na beannachdan (Blessings upon you),' said the minister.

'And to you,' said Hector. He seemed sad and quiet, watching the passengers. He suddenly said to the minister in Gaelic, 'Cur suas urnuigh air mo shon (Pray for me).'

For a moment he stood like a statue at the rail, gazing out at Naples, foreign, beautiful and pagan.

13

O N 18 and 19 March Hector had his interviews with
Lord Roberts at the War Office. The weather was
sharp and cold and London depressed him. Lord
Roberts received him coldly: he himself was happily married with
daughters (a son had been killed at Colenso in South Africa). He
found it distasteful to be involved in such a procedure, though
stories of Hector's unpopularity in Ceylon had reached him. He
himself had come from a good family, though he had never
been rich.

For Hector's part he remembered his first encounters with
Lord Roberts, the general adored by his troops in Afghanistan,
and who had recommended him for a commission. The now
cold eye of the general troubled him. The interviews took place
in a very formal atmosphere. The offences were ones which Lord
Roberts himself could hardly understand and for which he had a
special distaste.

'I will not make an exception for high rank,' he told Hector.
Sitting behind his desk, he seemed formidable and remote.

'Sir, may I—'

'There is nothing more to say, you will have to clear your
name or not, as the case may be. There appear to have been
many witnesses. I am determined to stamp out such offences if
they can be found to have occurred.'

'Sir, can I not be allowed to be retired from the army?'

'No, you can't, and in any case there would still be questions.'

'I could give private and personal circumstances as my reasons,
sir.'

'No, this has gone too far. The air must be cleared. You will have to return to Ceylon and face a court martial.'

For a moment Hector had a brief glimpse of glacial Afghanistan, of the cold dead eyes of the camels, of dead Afghan soldiers.

'I need hardly say how troublesome and indeed tragic I find this situation. I would never have envisaged such an interview. There has never been any question of your military qualities. But matters have gone too far, and the newspapers, as I understand it, have got hold of these stories. That is all.'

He seemed about to say something else but only shook his head angrily.

When Hector left the War Office, he walked for a while about the streets of London. After Ceylon he found the city cold, and he shivered now and again. His thoughts turned to Rootfield and to his brother William, and to the Highlands. Such accusations would appear horrifying to his own people.

He heard Roberts saying, 'The honourable thing—'

At a corner of a street he saw a man with one leg selling newspapers and clapping his hands against his body to keep warm. Soon perhaps his own tragic fall would be known. A cab passed; the horse looked weary and dispirited. Buildings of solid stone towered above him. The trees, such as he saw, had bare branches. A fat woman shouted at him to buy some flowers.

There is one more thing I have to do, he thought, and that will be the worst of all.

He felt as if he were in a dream, the more so when a man with a startlingly pale face marched up and down in front of him, now and again stopping to doff his hat with a deep flourish.

London, anonymous London, roared around him. Once he felt panic-stricken and clutched at a pillar. It was as if his body was becoming insubstantial in this centre of the Empire with its pulsating life. No one looked at him. Everyone walked past, eyes straight ahead as if fixed on an urgent destination.

He shivered more and more in the cold afternoon light among the banks and insurance offices of London, as spring fought its way towards summer, and youthful buds prepared to open.

Then he felt angry with Roberts. He could have been more

131

understanding than he had been. That cold remote eye had been the eye of an enemy.

I have served my country, he thought, and this is what happens. A man ought to be compensated for loneliness. A man is not inhuman.

The bodies of the hanged Afghans swayed in the cold wind of London. He saw an icy eye glaring down at him as he sat among the red theatre of soldiers. Then the Afghan became the straw man from which the straw gushed as the precise bayonet found its mark.

The following day he went to see his wife and son in Dulwich to which she had come apparently unmarried and pregnant many years before from a censorious Edinburgh. She was now thirty-five years old and he was fifty. Young Hector was sixteen. He had been sending money to have him educated at Dulwich College.

'I shan't be able to stay long,' he said, as if he were a stranger. 'I hope all is well with you.'

He looked round the comfortable but not lavishly furnished room. It seemed orderly enough and for a moment he felt a stab of pain. This domestic scene seemed desirable now.

Christine seemed remote and controlled. All of her younger, frothier ebullience had vanished, and there was a fine-boned maturity about her.

'I don't suppose you have any whisky?' Hector said.

'I'm afraid not. What are you doing in England?'

'I have some leave,' he said absently, 'and I thought I would call and see you. I have been in London.'

There was a little bare garden in front of the house in which a few twigs shook in the wind.

His son, still awkwardly adolescent, sat without speaking, now and again glancing at his mother. He had just put down a book which he had been reading.

Suddenly Hector said to his wife, 'Might I see you alone?' She nodded to young Hector, who left the room. As he did so his father said, 'Thank you, my boy,' but his son did not turn at the door.

The last time his father had seen him he had been in short trousers.

He is more like his mother than he is like me, thought Hector.

After the boy had left, the two sat in silence for a while, Christine very upright in her chair, straight-backed, her hands in her lap, so that it seemed as if she was being interviewed. Hector shifted his big body on the sofa, almost knocking over a blue vase which sat on a small table beside it.

'I wished to discuss my will with you,' he said.

She remained silent.

'Of course I have left what I have to you and the boy. There is some money. Have you a lawyer?'

'Mr Morrison,' she said. 'The family's solicitor in Edinburgh.'

'He will advise you, then. One never knows what may happen.'

'Is that why you came?'

'Yes.'

'Is anything wrong, then?'

'No, it is just that I am getting old and I feel that I wish to put my affairs in order. The other matter is, should anything happen, I wish for a private funeral without military honours.'

'You are very macabre. Are you suffering from some disease?'

'No, no disease.'

How odd, he thought, this room looks so military and orderly, nothing out of place in it. And yet at one time she used to be so careless and untidy.

'Are you sure you are telling me the whole truth? You seem preoccupied.'

I do not deserve to share my trouble with her, thought Hector. I have had little to do with her. There was my military world, and my beloved Arabs and my ideal boys. Perhaps she had always known that. When my son left the room that was perhaps the last time I shall see him. He felt restless again and in need of a drink.

'Would you like some tea?'

'No, thank you, I shall have to be leaving shortly.'

I am a passing stranger, and this is not the girl I knew. This

133

is a woman of formidable presence. A picture returned to him of her running from school on a shuttling day of April, with her books in her bag. He shut his eyes.

'I should like to leave you some money,' he said, taking some sovereigns from his wallet and leaving them on the small table beside the vase, which had some dry artificial flowers in it. She watched him in a severe silence. A brooch glowed on her brown dress. Her hair was gathered up in a bun. His restlessness increased. It was as if he couldn't keep still. He also felt too large for the room.

She looked at him shrewdly and said, 'I shall attend to these matters, do not fear, though perhaps there will be no immediate necessity.' But she knew that there was something wrong, she sensed it. In her obedient almost-widowhood, she had long lost her love – and there had never been much intimacy between them – but she recognised that he was troubled. His fists were clenched on his knees. His civilian suit didn't fit him, the arms seemed too long for the sleeve, and the breast too tight. His face, though tanned, was beginning to look old.

She was about to speak when he said suddenly, as if he could no longer bear to sit still, 'I must be going.'

'So soon?'

'Yes, I am afraid so. I am not in this country for long.'

'Very well, then. I shall take care of these matters.'

'Thank you,' he said quietly, and then, 'Goodbye then. Give my regards to the boy.'

After he had gone she sat in her chair for a while and then shouted, 'Hector, you can come in now. Your father has gone.'

When he came into the room she embraced him suddenly and fiercely, and said, 'We had a few matters to discuss. That was all.'

14

I N HIS dream he saw millions of eyes staring at him. After a while they steadied to the stars he had seen shining over the desert. When he woke up he felt strangely tranquil. He dressed and went for his breakfast in the large dining-room, sitting at a table by himself. After breakfast he walked into the drawing-room where the morning newspapers lay on a table. He scanned the headlines, then came to the front page of the European edition of the *New York Herald*. He read the words: GRAVE CHARGE LIES ON SIR HECTOR MACDONALD: NOT AMENABLE TO LAW IN CEYLON: HE SAILS TO ENGLAND TO MEET THE CHARGE.

He stood there for a moment in the same strange calm. Then he climbed the staircase and walked along the corridor to Room 105. He removed his jacket and hung it in the wardrobe. Then he took off his boots and put them under the bed. He looked into the mirror with an ironic smile. Then he took a small gun from his valise, put it to his head and pulled the trigger. His body toppled across the room, almost blocking the door, and lay in a growing pool of blood, mimicking as it were on the luxurious carpet the relentless spread of Empire.